P9-APQ-004

Edited by Douglas Glover

Best Canadian Stories 97

This book was written and published with the assistance of the Canada Council, the Ontario Arts Council and others. We acknowledge the support of the Canada Council for the Arts for our publishing program.

Acknowledgements: "Forde Abroad" by John Metcalf was first published in *The New Quarterly*. "California Cancer Journeys" by Mark Anthony Jarman first appeared in *McGill Street Magazine*. "Miss Pringle's Hour" by Cynthia Flood was originally published in *Descant*. "Horse from Persia" by Christian Petersen and "Remembering Manuel" by David Henderson originally appeared in *Grain*. "The Love of a Good Woman" by Alice Munro first appeared in *The New Yorker* (December 23-30, 1996).

ISBN 0 7780 1072 4 (hardcover)
ISBN 0 7780 1073 2 (softcover)
ISSN 0703 9476

Cover art by Henry Raeburn
Book design by Michael Macklem

Printed in Canada

PUBLISHED IN CANADA BY OBERON PRESS

When I was drawing together the stories for this collection, I kept thinking of a line from that movie *Joe vs. the Volcano.* Tom Hanks and Meg Ryan are standing on the lip of the volcano getting ready to jump in. Tom says, "What next?" And Meg replies, "You jump and you see."

For some reason, I felt less sure of myself than I have in the past, as if I had swum out beyond the marker buoys and found myself in an unknown channel. I read and read and these seven stories started to float up, to haunt the edges of my imagination in ways I find difficult to describe. Alice Munro, of course, can still nail a complex human emotion to the page with more elegant aplomb than any writer going. And it was a pure delight to discover John Metcalf furthering the adventures of his inimitable Canadian author-hero Robert Forde in "Forde Abroad." Every time I read Metcalf I am reminded of William Hazlitt's dictum: "Every word must be a blow." But what to say about Mark Jarman's fine dirge "California Cancer Journeys" with its gorgeous phrasing: "that last place of scalps and complicated slaughter?" Or David Henderson's disturbingly erotic tale of Anglo-colonial sexual corruption and murder set against the verdant jungles of El Salvador in "Remembering Manuel"—"When I opened the unlocked door, the putrid odour of decay hit me...?"

These are fresh, angular stories often speaking with peculiar voices that carry urgency and a version of truth in their own peculiarity (or particularity). And somehow it seems to me this particularity of voice is one of those things that makes a story good. So many times one reads a story that sounds as if it were trying to be a story: a good story strikes one as being nothing more than a voice that must be heard. And so we have Cynthia Flood's "Miss Pringle's Hour," the terse diaries and memoranda of a boarding-school headmistress valiantly warding off despair with outmoded principles and starched routine. And Ramona Dearing's offbeat, minimalist charm in "Love Bites and Little Spanks"—"She leans forward across the table and talks soft. 'How about a three-way?' She wiggles her eyebrows. 'Before bingo or after?' I ask." And Christian

Petersen's brilliant one-paragraph flight of fancy, "Horse from Persia, the last-minute lament of Alexander J. Hare"—"Hanging is a kindness that's somewhat hard for me to understand, and harder to thank you for and smile...."

Douglas Glover

Contributions for the twenty-eighth volume, published or unpublished, should be sent to Oberon Press, 400–350 Sparks Street, Ottawa, Ontario, K1R 7S8 before 30 November, 1997. All manuscripts should be accompanied by a stamped self-addressed envelope.

The following magazines were consulted: *The Antigonish Review, Blood & Aphorisms, Canadian Author, Canadian Fiction Magazine, Canadian Forum, The Capilano Review, Descant, Event, The Fiddlehead, Geist, grain, Malahat Review, The New Quarterly, The New Yorker, Nimrod, Paragraph, Prairie Fire, Quarry, Saturday Night* and *Windsor Review.*

Forde Abroad

John Metcalf

Roast pork with crackling was repellent. Roast pork with crackling was *goyishe dreck*. Black Forest ham with Swiss cheese was, however, her favourite kind of sandwich. She loved even the greasiest of salamis. Sausages, on the other hand, were unclean. All Chinese food involving pork was perfectly acceptable with the single exception of steamed minced pork which was, apparently, vile *trayf* of the most abhorrent kind. Prosciutto she adored. But pork chops... *feh*!

Forde stared at Sheila in exasperation.

"And you can be sure they haven't changed," she said, "in their hearts."

"But how do you know they ever *were*...."

"How do you know they weren't?"

"Well, I don't, but how *could* they have deported any-one? Slovenia was invaded by the Nazis. The Slovenians were a subject people. Slovenia was an occupied country just as—as France was."

"And look at *their* record."

"I don't think," he said, "that this is a particularly logical conversation."

Lines at the corners of her eyes tightened.

"So what makes you think they didn't collaborate? Like the whatnames."

"Which whatnames?"

"The French ones. Begins with M."

"The *milice*?"

"Exactly."

"Well, I *don't* know...."

"More likely than not, I'd say."

"...but I'll look it up," he said.

She bent over the atlas again.

"Here's the Nazis immediately north of them in Austria. And then immediately to the right of them in Hungary— what were those called? The Iron Cross? The Iron Guard?"

"I think it was the Arrowcross."

With her left shoulder she gave a quick, irritated shrug.

"And then *here* to the south of them you've got the Us-tashi in Croatia. Why *should* the Slovenians have been any different?"

"Listen," he said, "Sheila...."

"But, please," she said, "it's your career. I know I'm just being silly."

She patted below her eyes with a tissue.

"If it's what you want, off you go."

She sniffed.

"Off you go," she said, her voice breaking.

"Sheila...*please.*"

"No!" she said fiercely. "No! You can go there and you can do what you want. I don't care. I don't *care* if you choose to consort with Slovenians."

To her offended and retreating back, he said, "I hardly think the word 'consort' is quite...oh, *indescribable* BALLS!"

After she had left for work, Forde stood over the toilet in the second-floor bathroom. The intense, rich yellow, the dayglo brightness of his urine, gave him daily pleasure. The vitamins did it. He wasn't sure if it were the E, the Beta Carotene, the C, or the Megavits. He had read in a newspaper article that vitamins C and E "captured free radicals"; he had no idea what that meant and wasn't curious but he enjoyed the sound of it. It made him think of warfare against insurgent forces in fetid jungles, sibilant native blades, *parang* and *kris.*

Even the toilet itself pleased him. It was probably sev-enty or eighty years old. Against the back of the bowl in purple script was the word "Vitreous." And above that in a wreath of what might have been acanthus leaves was the toilet's name—"Prompto."

He flushed the toilet and watched his brightness diluted, swirled away. He stood looking at himself in the medicine cabinet mirror as the plumbing groaned and water rilled and spirted, silence rising, settling.

He wandered into his frowsty study and sat at his ugly government-surplus oak desk. Beyond its far edge the scabby radiator. Then the blank wall. Two years earlier he had faced the window but had spent too much time gazing out watching passers-by and the busyness of dogs.

Usually he enjoyed the daily solitude and drew the deepening silence of the house around him like a blanket. But on this day the silence burdened him. He sat looking down at the gold-plated stem-winder which always lay flat on the desk to his right. He wound it every morning, pleased every morning by the feel of the knurled winding-knob. He had bought it at a pawn shop cheaply because engraved on the back of the watch were the words:

Presented to George Pepper in recognition of forty-five years service to the Canadian Cardboard Box Company.

It amused him to think that this was the only presentation gold watch he'd ever have. No such flourishes were likely to conclude *his* career. He kept the watch on the desk as a talisman, a spur to effort, as *memento mori*, as a reminder of the world to which he gratefully did not belong. He thought of the watch as "George." He sometimes talked to it.

This is a lovely bit of writing, George, even if I say so myself. And why not? No-one else will.

I think we can get another hour in, George, before we're completely knackered.

He wound the watch.

He sighed.

He sat staring across his desk's familiar clutter. He had no appetite for writing necessary letters, for providing references and recommendations, for the fiddle of filing. His last novel was now six months behind him—almost a year since he'd written seriously—but he remained listless, uncommitted about what he might do next, bored.

When he was in the grip of first-draft writing, he risked nothing that might break the flow. Ritual and omen ruled. He laid in stocks of Branston Pickle, wooden matches, tins of *Medaglio d'Oro*. His heart leapt at the cawing of crows. He did not like to leave the house, did not open his mail, did not shower, wash, or shave, slept in unchanged shirt and underpants, sat in his study smelling the smell of himself.

It was only on Friday mornings that this obsessive routine was interrupted. On Friday mornings the cleaning lady hired by Sheila arrived at nine and made his life unendurable until noon. He had begged and remonstrated, but Sheila had offered as the only alternative that he clean the house himself as she had neither the time nor energy. And definitely no inclination. He saw fully the justice of her position but felt put upon.

He attempted politeness when he let the woman in, attempted conversations about the weather, the heat, the cold, the damp, but could never understand more than a word in five of anything she said. Although he closed his study door and put on his industrial ear-mufflers, he could still hear her imprecations and mad Portuguese diatribes, her crooning monologues punctuated by sudden squawks and screeches directed at vacuum cleaner or doorknob.

She had once left a note on the kitchen counter which read:

Mis mis erclen finisples.

It had worried at him most of the afternoon.

Sheila had read it with impatient ease. *Miss. Mister Clean is finished, please.*

According to Sheila, Mrs. Silva had an unemployed husband with three toes missing on one foot from an industrial accident, a son who was a bad lot, and was herself a devoutly Catholic hypochondriac whose spare time was divided equally between her priest and doctor.

He could not understand how Sheila had found any of this out, how she understood anything the bloody woman said, but he had come to suspect that Sheila's ability to understand Mrs. Silva, bereaved Romanian upholsterers, and monoglot Vietnamese shelf-stockers in odoriferous Asian stores was less to do with some rare linguistic talent than it was to do with the fact that she was a nicer person than he was.

He started to link up the doodles.

One of John D. MacDonald's thrillers came into his mind. He'd always admired the title: *The Girl, the Gold Watch, and Everything*.

He was supposed to be polishing an interview which was supposed to appear in the summer issue of *Harvest*, but *Harvest* was doubtless two issues behind where it was supposed to be so that all of its three hundred subscribers would have to wait with bated breath until the summer of *next* year before they could devour his profound and penetrating insights into this, that, and whatever, so that, all in all, six of this and half a dozen of the other, all things being equal, when push came to shove, polishing the bloody thing up did not seem an enterprise

"...of great pith and moment"

he declaimed into the study's silence.

Who *said* that?

Fortinbras?

Hamlet himself?

He plodded downstairs to find a copy of *The Complete Plays* and to make a cup of tea. Better for his health, Sheila insisted, than coffee.

I must put my pyjamas, he chanted, *in the drawer marked pyjamas*.

I must eat my charcoal biscuit, he recited, *which is good for me*.

As he stood waiting for the kettle to boil, he looked at the *New York Times Atlas of the World* Sheila had left open on the counter. He took a roll of Magic Tape from the kitchen drawer and started to tape up the tears in the tattered blue dust-jacket; he'd been meaning to do that for weeks. Often after dinner they sat over the atlas finishing the wine and squabbling happily over holidays they would never be able to afford. Sheila's most recent creation had been a trip up the Nile to see the temples but without getting off the boat because Egypt was hot and smelly and every historical site was plagued by importunate dragomen, smelly and anti-semites to a man, and one could surely get a *sense* of the temples while remaining in one's deck chair and being served large Bombay Gin martinis.

A snort of laughter escaped him as he thought of the words *"consort with Slovenians."*

Her performance that morning had not, of course, been about Slovenians, World War II fascist groups or deported Jews. It had been what he thought shrinks called "displacement." It was that, simply, she was upset that he was going away and although she had not yet said so, she was even more upset that at the conference he would for the first time be meeting Karla.

Sheila did not like Karla. She had taken against her from the arrival of the first letter. She always referred to her as "your Commie pen-pal."

The conference was to be held in the Alps at a lake resort called Splad. The brochure about the hotel and its services was written in an English which charmed him. He thought it strange that in a communist country a hotel would offer to launder silk handkerchiefs; they also offered to launder Gentlemen Linen and Nightshirsts. He had studied the sample menus with fascination; he particularly liked the sound of National Beans with Pork Jambs. It seemed certain that the whole expedition would provide him with unimaginable comic material.

But he had scarcely bothered to glance at the program itself when it had arrived from the Literary and Cultural Association of Slovenia, disliking the hairy East European paper it was printed on and the fact that the paper was not the normal 8 1/2 by 11 inches but 8 1/2 by 11 3/4, an intensely irritating deviation probably traceable, like the metric system, to the meddling of Napoleon.

From horrid experience, he knew that the papers would range from deconstructionist babble to weird explications in uncertain English of the profundities of Mazo de la Roche and Lucy Maud Montgomery.

Not that he would be caught listening to any of it; he would rather, he thought, sit and listen to a washing machine.

And ranged between the deconstructionists and the simply uncomprehending there would be interminable feminists in frocks and army boots, gay theorists in bright green leather shoes, huddles of Slovenians in suits discussing Truth, the State, the Writer, smart-aleck Marxist smarty boots, chaps in tweed from New Zealand....

But looking on the bright side, his expenses in Slovenia would be covered by the Literary and Cultural Association, and his travel expenses to Slovenia would be covered by the Department of External Affairs which was also to pay him a *per diem* and a small honorarium. This, together with another honorarium from the Slovenians for reading, might mean returning home five hundred dollars ahead.

And he'd be freed from his desk, from the chipped radiator, the blank wall facing; he'd be free of the house, he'd be out and about, out in the world, free of the weight of his numbing routines.

His spirits rose at the thought of leaving behind the wearying end of Ottawa's winter, the snow beginning now its slow retreat revealing Listerine bottles and dog turds. He would be leaving behind brown bare twigs and flying toward a world in leaf, in the alpine meadows, gentians.

And once ensconced in Splad, he would perhaps meet someone who would wish to write about his work. Perhaps a convivial evening in the bar might lead to further translation.... Nor could he deny that he enjoyed the attention, couldn't deny that it made him feel expansive to answer questions, pontificate, disparage Robertson Davies.

"What I don't understand," Sheila had said, probing at his contradictions to deflate and anger him in these last bickering days before his flight, "what I can't follow is why it gives you pleasure to impress people for whom you have little or no respect. Why *is* that?"

"Well, it's not so much the *people*," he'd explained, "it's what they represent."

"And what's that?"

"Well…a certain interest, a respect even…these are academics from all over the world, you know."

"And according to you some of them can't speak English and the rest talk gibberish."

"I'm not saying it's a *desirable* situation, Sheila, but one's reputation rests to a certain extent on how much attention academics pay to one's work."

"One's reputation does, does it?"

He had shaken his head slowly to convey a weary dignity.

"And one doesn't feel," she'd probed further, "that disporting oneself in front of people one disdains is rather… well…*pitiable*?"

He sighed and sipped at the tea.

Lighted a luxurious cigarette.

Closed the atlas.

And there also awaited in Splad the pleasure of holding in his hands a translation into Serbian of his third novel, *Winter Creatures*. His translator was travelling to Splad from Belgrade bringing the book with him. At a conference two years earlier in Italy he'd been approached by a man—and actually he wouldn't swear to the *absolute* details of any of this because he'd been rather drunk himself and had not quite grasped everything the man was saying what with the noise in the bar and the accent and the syntax—by a man whose father was Serbian and whose mother was Croatian— or possibly it was the other way round—who worked for a cultural radio station and magazine in Belgrade and who was an actor and impresario who translated works in English into Serbian on behalf of the Writers of Serbia Cultural Association and who, when not involved in manifestations, worked by day as chauffeur to a man of extensive power.

After his return to Canada, Forde had largely forgotten this loud stranger with his winks and nods, his glittering gold fillings, his finger tapping the side of his nose, until the telephone calls began.

Ripped from sleep at 3:33, heart pounding, staring into the digital clock inches from his face, Forde croaked into the phone.

"Hello?" he repeated.

"Here is Drago."

"Who?"

"Drago! Drago!"

"Who is it?"

He flapped his hand at her.

3:34

"You will visit me in Beograd. We will have much talking."

"Beograd?"

"Yes! Yes, Robert Forde."

"Excuse me...you're...from Bologna?"

"Yes, *certainly* Bologna."

"I'm sorry. For a moment, I...ah...rather disoriented."

3.35

"In Beograd we will together drink Nescafé."

This had been the first of many calls.

All came in the small hours.

"Get *his* fucking number!" hissed Sheila, furiously humping the sheets over her shoulder. "I'll phone *him* in the middle of *his* fucking night, fucking Slav fuckheads."

Forde soon came to dread that ruthless, domineering voice. Drago bombarded, hectored, rode roughshod.

He was implacable.

He was impervious.

"Here is Drago. You have written: 'American students littered the steps.' This *littered* is not a nice word, not a *possible* word, it is meaning *excrement* and *rubbish* and so would *offend* the Americans so we find a *compromise* word...."

He wondered what the book would look like. He presumed it would be a paperback but didn't know whether they went in for the quality paperback format or whether they produced paperbacks in the utilitarian French style. He realized that he didn't even know if Serbian was written in the Roman alphabet or in Cyrillic. He wondered what Serbian readers would make of *Winter Creatures* given Drago's strange queries and frequent assurances that he would "make things come nice." He suspected that the novel had been less translated than traduced. So why was

17

he so gratified to have his novel badly translated into a language he couldn't read?

Forde did not delude himself.

He had not forgotten the wellingtons phone call.

"Wellies," said Drago. "This means, I think, *venery*."

"*What?*"

"You *know*, Robert Forde, what I am saying."

"No, *no*, Drago! Wellies are rubber boots."

He had listened to the echoic international silence.

"Short for wellingtons."

"Never," said Drago, "in all my reading and my talking, *never* have I heard it called so."

"*It?*" he'd squeaked.

But he *was* gratified. As he sat doodling at his desk, he hummed. Had he liked cigars, he would have smoked one. Had there been a mirror in his study, he would have inclined his head with all the benign courtesy of a grandee.

"...consort with Slovenians...."

He grinned at the radiator.

He was even pleased by Sheila's moody assaults, pleased and a little flattered that after all the years they'd been together she could still flame into jealousy. Not that she had the slightest cause for concern. As he'd told her repeatedly, his friendship with Karla was a purely literary friendship.

Her first letter had arrived some three years ago from the University of Jena in the German Democratic Republic. She had expressed her admiration of his novels—a colleague at the University of Augsburg had lent her some volumes— and although her syntax and vocabulary were sometimes peculiar, he'd been pleased to receive her praise. No-one from East Germany had ever written to him before. She had ended her letter by saying that her great sorrow was that she had not been able to read his first two novels because she could not obtain them. Was it possible he could send her copies? For such a resolution of the problem she would be most grateful.

"Why has it always got to be *you*?" Sheila demanded. "Why should *you* have to pay for the books and postage?"

"Well, I've never thought about it before but I don't

18

think their currency trades. They can't buy things with it in the west."

"Well how did her letter get here then with an East German stamp on it?"

"I don't know. I don't know how that works."

"Well," said Sheila. "I'd say there's something suspicious about it."

He had sent her the books and within weeks they were writing back and forth regularly. What other Canadian writers should she read? Who were reliable critics? Which books were most loved by the Canadian people? She loved to read about Red Indians and Eskimos and the North. Was Grey Owl thought a great Canadian writer? Canadians, as she had studied in Margaret Atwood's book *Survival*, had invented the genre of the wild animal story. Should she read Ernest Thompson Seton? An anthology at the University contained an Ernest Thompson Seton story entitled "Raggylug, the Story of a Cottontail Rabbit." Was this one of his most loved stories?

Forde had dealt with all this misplaced enthusiasm firmly. He had explained that no books were beloved of the Canadian people with the sole exception of *Anne of Green Gables* and that only because it had been on television. Most Canadians, he had explained, were functionally illiterate. No stories by Ernest Thompson Seton were "most loved" because only academics knew who he was.

He explained that most Eskimos worked in collectives with power tools turning out soapstone seals. The North was actually a vast slum run by the federal government's Canadian Mortgage and Housing Corporation, the landscape littered with empty oil barrels. There *were* Red Indians but no longer of the bow-and-arrow variety. They were not to be called "Red" Indians. Indeed, they were not to be called "Indians." In Ottawa, people of the First Nations wearing traditional braids and cowboy boots were almost bound to be high-priced, hotshot lawyers.

He began to send her reading lists; in the library he xeroxed what critical articles he could stomach; he sent clippings and reviews. When he went out walking around

Ottawa's used-book stores, he picked up inexpensive paperbacks and from time to time sent parcels.

After a few months had gone by, he felt bold enough to start correcting her English.

The more he moulded and shaped her, the larger the claims her letters made on him. She became increasingly confident of his attention. Her ardent engagement with his own writing slightly embarrassed him. It seemed a natural progression for his letters to move from *Sincerely* to *With best wishes* to *With warm regards* to *Affectionately*. He had hesitated before writing *With love* and had then delayed mailing the letter.

During the two weeks he waited for her reply he found that the letter and her possible reactions to it came often into his mind.

He asked no questions about her life but often as he sat staring across the grain of the government-surplus desk made uglier by thick polyurethane, he found himself wandering, daydreaming.

He had gleaned some few facts about her. He imagined that she must be between 35 and 40 because she had a son aged ten. She had not mentioned a husband; when she used the word "we" she always seemed to mean she and the boy. She lived in an apartment in an old house. She used the spare bedroom as her study.

When Sheila commented on the flow of letters from the German Democratic Republic, he had explained to her that such contacts were simply a normal part of the literary life, a necessary part of the shape of a career.

After they had been corresponding for about a year, there arrived in the week before Christmas a padded airmail package fastened in European style with split brass pins. It contained between two sheets of cardboard a photograph of Karla and a Christmas card drawn by Viktor of the Three Magi and what was probably a camel.

The photograph was a glossy close-up studio portrait in black and white and lighted in a stilted and old-fashioned style. Karla was in dramatic profile gazing up toward the upper left-hand corner. It reminded Forde of a Hollywood publicity photo from the forties of some such star as Joan Crawford or Myrna Loy.

Embarrassed that Sheila should see it, he said, "What a strange thing to send someone!"

"Fancies herself, doesn't she?" said Sheila.

"But going to a *studio*," said Forde.

Sheila tilted the photo.

"Probably air-brushed," she said, dropping it on the counter.

Pointing at the camel, he said, "What do you think that is?"

"I just wonder," she said, "what you'll get next."

What he got next was a request for three tubes of Revlon Color Stay lipstick: No. 41 *Blush*, No. 04 *Nude*, and No. 42 *Flesh*. He had lurked along the cosmetics counters in Eaton's in the Rideau Centre trying to avoid the eye of any of their attendant beauticians. He knew these supercilious women with their improbable sculpted makeup thought him a pervert, the Eaton's equivalent of the schoolyard's man-in-a-mac. He had felt uncomfortable and faintly guilty while buying the lipsticks but later felt even guiltier about not telling Sheila.

But he had done no wrong. He had to insist on that. It was not being disloyal to describe Sheila as in certain ways excitable. There was simply no point in upsetting her needlessly. Where lay the fault in buying small gifts for a friend—a colleague—who lived under a repressive totalitarian regime which did not allow her access to such simple commodities as lipstick? Or the *Ysatis* perfume by Givenchy she'd later requested?

He opened his desk drawer and took out the calendar. He had put the photograph inside the calendar to keep it flat. He looked at the upturned face. He looked at the dark fall of hair. Her lips were slightly parted. Light glistened on the fullness of her bottom lip. It was as if seconds before the photographer had pressed the shutter-release button, she had run her tongue across her lip wetting it.

He put the photograph back in the calendar.

Tearing off the doodles page from his writing pad and

the page beneath where the ink had gone through, he
started to jot down all the words in German he could think
of. He couldn't think of many. He arranged them into al-
phabetic order and sat looking at the result.

autobahn	Kristallnacht
Blitz	Luftwaffe
dankeschön	Panzer
ersatz	Realpolitik
flak	Reich
Fuehrer	Stalag
Gauleiter	Übermensh
Gestapo	Waffen SS
Kaiser	auf Wiedersehen

Sheila was pretending to be concentrating on driving. From
Ottawa International Airport he was to fly to Toronto on
the Air Canada Rapidair service. In Toronto he was to
board a Lufthansa flight to Frankfurt. In Frankfurt he was
to board a JAT flight for Slovenia's capital, Ljubljana. He
stared out of the window at the wastes of snow, the frozen
trees, the roadside lines of piled crud left by the snowplow.
From time to time Sheila sniffed.

"All this stuff's of your own imagining, you know."

She did not reply.

"Sheila?"

"I've said what I had to say, thank you."

"Yes, but it was untrue and unfair."

As the road curved round to the parking and departures
area, Sheila said, "I'll drop you off at the Air Canada counters and then I won't have to bother with parking."

"And also," he said, "hurtful."

She pulled the car in to the kerb and parked.

"Well...," said Forde.

"Have a good trip," she said.

"Aren't you going to kiss me goodbye?"

She inclined her head toward him and he found his lips
brushing her cheek.

He gathered his carry-on bag, umbrella and briefcase

and opening the car door said, "Really, Sheila, you're being ridiculous."

She sat staring ahead.

He got out and shut the door.

Stood for a moment.

Started across the sidewalk to the revolving door.

Sheila leaned across the passenger seat and wound down the window. She called out to him.

"Pardon?"

"*Az der putz shtait....*"

"What?"

"*Az der putz shtait ligt doss saichel in tuchus.*"

"What's that mean?"

She turned the key in the ignition.

"*What did that mean?*"

He reached for the door handle.

She pushed down the button locking all the doors.

He banged on the roof of the car with the flat of his hand.

She rolled up the window.

"*I demand to know what that meant!*"

A small male child with a suitcase on wheels stopped to gape up at him.

A Blue Line cab driver parked behind them had lowered his window and was staring.

"*What did that mean?*"

He emphasized each word by accompanying it with a bash on the car's hood with the malacca handle of his umbrella.

The taxi driver started honking his horn.

Sheila stretched across the passenger seat and opened the window two or three inches. Hoisting the strap of the carry-on bag higher on his shoulder and jamming the briefcase under his arm, Forde stooped to confront her through the narrow slot.

"It's an old Yiddish saying."

Forde glared.

"*Az der putz shtait...* When the prick stands up," she said,

"...*ligt doss saichel in tuchus*... the brains sink into the ass."

The ornate iron lamp-posts along the lake's margin speared light out on the water. Gravel crunched under their feet. Somewhere out beyond the reach of the lamps a waterfowl beat a brief commotion in the water. After the heat and the blare and the smoke of the crowded bars in the dining-room, the breeze from the lake smelled invigoratingly boggy.

"Intrigue," continued Christopher, "will be rampant."

He wiggled his fingers like fishes.

"Aswirl with currents."

"But who's listening? Does anyone really *care* what academics say?"

"*Everybody* is listening, Robert. This isn't Canada. Much of what's going on here you won't be able to understand. But the Party is listening, the factions of the separatists are listening, the Croatians are listening, the Serbs, the Macedonians, a positive *stew* of intelligence people.... And there are Slovenian writers here, too. They're important political figures, spokespeople. You see, writing here *is* politics."

With Christopher Harris, Forde felt he had hit the motherlode. They had sat together on the bus which had carried the party from the Ljubljana Holiday Inn to Splad and had quickly fallen into delighted conversation. Christopher was, Forde assumed, gay, about Forde's age, his nose blooming with drink-burst veins, and his fingernails all bitten to the quick. He was a British expatriate who lived and taught in Lund in Sweden—*Provincial. Something of a backwater of a university, really. I'm suited*—but who was an expert on all things Yugoslavian. His passion in life was the celebration of Slovenia and the Slovene language; he had translated most of the significant literature; he was working on a history.

Slovenians, Christopher had explained, considered themselves strongly European, a civilized, energetic northern people distinct from the increasingly dubious rabble to be found to the south, a rabble which culminated in the barbarism and squalor of Islam. This did not mean, Christopher had insisted, that the Slovenians were any more racist than anyone else. Exactly the same sentiments were openly expressed in Germany, France and Italy. Try cashing a cheque issued in Rome in a bank in Milan without having to listen to an earful about the duplicity of idle southern monkeys.

Christopher had also explained that although the ostensible purpose of the conference was to discuss matters Canadian, much of the international presence was also intended by the organizers as a buffer and defence for separatist Slovenians who would slant their papers and statements in politically unacceptable directions.

Secession was in the air.

They turned back toward the hotel, Christopher sparkling off fact and anecdote—Saint Cyril, called in earlier life Constantine, the Glagolitic alphabet, the battles of Kosovo and Lepanto, the quirks of Selim the Terrible, the westernmost reaches of the Ottoman Empire, the karst cave system near Ljubljana, Chetniks, fourteenth-century church frescos—pausing only to sing sad stanzas from a Slovenian folksong about boys leaving their sweethearts to suffer their forced military service in the Austro-Hungarian army.

"'Alf a mo', Squire," he said in a sudden Cockney whine.

He stood with his back to Forde and pissed loudly on a bush.

Forde suddenly felt shivery cold and quite drunk.

The verb "to stale" came into his mind.

He had had some powerful short brown drinks commended by Christopher and two bottles of nasty wine.

Christopher's feet on the gravel again.

"That mansion set back there," he said, pointing, "was one of ex-King Peter's summer palaces. Do you know Cecil Parrott? Chap who translated *The Good Soldier Svejk* for Penguin? When he was a young man, he was tutor in that house to the two Crown Princes. Tiny, the literary world, isn't it?"

The bulk of the hotel was looming in the darkness. It was a strange building, its central block the remains of a massively-built castle which according to Christopher dated from the fifteenth century. In the nineteen-thirties, an architect had joined onto the existing structure three huge concrete and glass wings. They rose up into the air like birds' wings, rather like, Forde thought, three immense upside down Stealth aircraft. The castle part was divided up into a reception area, kitchens, and a variety of bedrooms on different confusing levels and up and down small stone stairways. The three concrete and glass wings contained most of the bedrooms and an auditorium, conference rooms, and the vast dining-room which was cantilevered out over the lake's edge.

"So as the Nazis withdrew," Christopher was saying, "the only organized force able to step in was the communists. But they'd been a military force, a partisan force, there was no *civil* organization. So inevitably there was great civil confusion. It was a sad period. The communist peasants went on the rampage. The churches, of course, took the brunt of it. Paintings, carvings, tapestries...so much of it smashed and put to the torch...so many beautiful things lost forever."

He sighed.

"To them, of course," he said, "it was nothing but capitalist trumpery."

Forde stopped and put his hand on Christopher's arm. He was overcome by a sudden warmth of feeling. With the earnestness and grave courtesy of the inebriated, Forde said, "That is the first time in my life, Christopher, that I have heard the word 'trumpery' used in conversation."

"And you are the first person I have met," said Christopher, "to whom I could have said it *secure*," raising his forefinger for emphasis, "*secure* in the knowledge it would be understood."

They crunched on toward the hotel.

Forde's room was in the warren of rooms in the castle part of the hotel. He had been in and out of it three times now since arriving at Splad that afternoon but was still uncertain of his route. He knew that he had to make a first turn left at the painting of the dead deer.

The corridors, staircases, and walled-in embrasures were hung with *Nature morte de chasse* paintings. Early to mid-nineteenth century, most of them, he thought, though a few might have been earlier. It was a genre he'd always avoided, disliking the lavishing of such formidable technique on the depiction of wounds. There was something unsettling about the best of the paintings. He sensed in them a sexual relishing of cruelty and death. He felt repelled in the same way by what he thought of as the Mayan element in Mexican crucifixes, Christ's wounds shown to the white of the bone, shocking atavistic inlays of ivory.

He bent to peer at the small brass plate at the bottom of the frame but all it said was: 1831.

The deer was lying head down across a rustic bench. Two tensely seated hounds with mad eyes yearned up at it. In its nostrils, blood.

As he walked on down the silent corridor, he found himself groping for the name of Queen Victoria's favourite painter. The man whose animal paintings had got nastier and nastier, the cruelty coming closer to the surface, until his mind gave way entirely and he'd died years later barking mad. The man who did the lions at the foot of Nelson's monument in Trafalgar Square, the *Stag at Bay* man.

It was on the tip of his tongue
Began with "L."
Lutyens?

Battues of grouse and pheasants. A gralloched deer. Hecatombs of rabbits, grouse, partridges, snipe and ducks. In some of the paintings, for no obvious reason, greaves, helms, gorgets, a polished steel cuirass inlaid with brass, a drum bright with regimental crest and colours amid the piled, limp bodies.

He had to go up a short flight of stone steps just after a painting of a dead hawk and rabbit hanging upside down from a fence. Highlights glinted on the rabbit's eye and on the hawk's curved talons. The rabbit's grey fur was wind-ruffled to show the soft blue underfur pocked where pellets had struck, each swollen puncture dark with gore.

At the top of the steps he turned the wrong way. The short curving corridor terminated in a dead-end. He stood in the stone embrasure staring at the ice-making machine.

It rumbled and hummed.

"Landseer!" he exclaimed. "Sir Edwin Landseer."

He followed the corridor in the opposite direction and, recognizing the red brocade curtains partially drawn across the entrance to the recess, finally gained his room.

He felt relieved to lock his door. It had been a long day and he felt tired and crammed with undigested new experience. The bedroom had an antique look, the furniture old and heavy, the walls covered in some kind of grey material, slightly furry to the touch, velvet perhaps. Off the bedroom to the left was a bathroom and to the right a separate little room intended perhaps as a dressing-room. It contained a chest of drawers and a long mirror in a gilt frame. He had been pleased to discover in what had seemed to be a cupboard, a TV set and a mini-bar.

The thing Forde loathed most about travelling was *carrying things*. He hated lugging heavy cases about. He hated luggage itself. Luggage, he had often proposed to Sheila as she sat on her case to get it to close, reduced people to being its ill-tempered guardians. Who would wish to stand with the anxious herd watching tons of luggage tumbling onto carousels? Who would wish to share in that mesmerized silence as luggage trundled round and round?

Forde travelled only with a carry-on bag. He never carried more than two shirts, two pairs of underpants and two pairs of socks. Sheila made up for him little Saran Wrap packages of Tide, each secured with a garbage-bag tie and each sufficient to do one wash. Every night he washed his clothes in the washbasin, scrubbing clean the collars and cuffs of the shirts with an old toothbrush, and then hung everything over the bath to dry.

He lay in the dark letting his mind run back over the last two days to his landing in Ljubljana. Thought of his surprise at seeing booths at the airport for Avis and Hertz. At the taxi which accepted Visa and on whose tape deck the Stones were singing "Midnight Rambler." At the opulence of the Ljubljana Holiday Inn. Hardly the grim face of God-less Communism he'd been looking forward to.

It had all been much like anywhere else.

He'd wandered the streets of the old city, the buildings distinguished but shabby, the river running through the centre of it all, graceful bridges, churches and nuns every-where, the castle at the top of the hill boarded up because of the danger of falling masonry, no money Christopher told him later for renovation or repair.

But there was certainly money in the new part of the city. Most shop doors carried Visa and American Express stickers. Familiar names in windows—Black and Decker, Cuisinart, Braun. Parked along the streets, Audi, BMW, Volkswagen. In a bookstore window he'd seen translations of Jack Higgins, Wilbur Smith, Sidney Sheldon, Dick Francis, and, to his mortification, an omnibus edition of three Jalna novels by Mazo de la Roche.

But the play of pictures in his mind kept going back to the taxi ride in from the airport. Woods. Small fields. Groups of men and women working in what he took to be allotments of some kind. A tethered donkey eating the roadside grass. In a vegetable garden, a woman working with a mattock.

Then a narrow stone humpback bridge, the road rising, and he'd been looking down over the side of the bridge into a meadow. And there he'd caught a flash of an enormous white bird standing.

He'd cried out to the driver to stop and back up. He'd pointed. The driver, rolling down his window and lighting a cigarette, said, "You like such?"

He'd sat staring.

"What is it? What's it called?"

The driver said something, perhaps a name.

Mist hung over the stream. He could not see the water. The stream's course was plotted by polled willows. The bird was taller than the three grey stacked bales of last year's hay. He guessed it stood nearly four feet high.

"Cranes," Christopher had said on the bus from Ljubl-jana. "I've somehow never really *warmed* to birds."

"Not storks?"

"No, these are rather famous. They'll have been here for about two weeks now. They spend the winters in North Africa. Morocco, somewhere like that."

"And they nest here? In Slovenia?"

"And always in the same place. They just pile new stuff on top of the old."

"You mean the same birds go back to the same nest?"

"They mate for life, apparently. Some pairs have been together for fifty years."

He pulled a face.

"Not really my cup of tea."

As he slipped toward sleep just conscious of the irregular dripping sounds from his shirt in the bathroom, he imagined himself in the meadow trying to get closer to the crane without frightening it. The bird was aware of him and walked away keeping the distance between them constant. It walked slowly and gracefully, sometimes hesitating before settling down a foot, reminding him of the way herons stalk. He could see it quite clearly. Its body was white except for the bustle of tail feathers about its rump which were grey shading to black. Its long neck was black with a white patch around the eyes and on top of its head a cap of brilliant red. He edged closer. The crane was pacing along the margin of the mist, from time to time stopping and turning its head to the side as if listening. Past the old bales of hay and the field becoming squelchy, breaking down into tussocks and clumps. And as he looks up again from the unsure footing, the crane is stepping into the mist which accepts it and wreathes around it, hiding it from view.

Three waiters in mauve jackets and mauve bow ties stood beside the buffet tables impassively surveying the breakfasters. Their function seemed to be to keep the tables stocked and tidy. From time to time they flapped their napkins at crumbs. Two of them had luxuriant drooping mustachios, growths he thought of as Serbian.

He inspected the array of dishes. Cornflakes, muesli, pickled mushrooms, sliced ham, salami, liverwurst, hard-boiled eggs, smoked fish, triangles of processed Swiss cheese in silver foil, a soft white cheese in liquid—either feta or brinza—and small round cheeses covered in yellow wax which he suspected might be kashkaval—honey, rolls, butter. Juice in jugs. Milk. Coffee in thermos flasks.

No sign of Christopher so he took his tray to an un-crowded table and nodded to a darkly Arab-looking man who promptly passed him a card which read: Abdul-Rahman Majeed Al-Mansoor. Baghdad. Iraq.

"Hello," said Abdul-Rahman. "How are you? I am fine."

As Forde started to crack and peel shell from his egg, the other man at the table took out his wallet and extracted a card, saying, "I hope that my coughing will not discommode you. I cannot suppress it as the cough is hysterical in origin. My card. Dorscht. Vienna. Canadianist."

Pretending abstraction, Forde busied himself with his breakfast. Covertly he watched Dorscht. Dorscht had a black plastic thermos jug from which he was pouring...hot water. He was wearing a leather purse or pouch on a strap which crossed his chest. The archaic word "scrip" flashed into Forde's mind. From his purse Dorscht took a cracker, a Ryvita-looking thing, and started nibbling.

The hubbub in the room was rising to a constant roar. Three men and two women brought trays to the table. They seemed to be a mixture of Canadians and Americans and all seemed to know each other. They were arguing about a poet.

"...but surely he's *noted* for his deconstruction of binaries."

"...and by the introduction of chorus avoids the monological egocentricity of conventional lyric discourse."

Christ!

"Let me say," brayed one of the men, "let me say, in full awareness of heteroglossia...."

Christ!

Dorscht performed his chugging cough.

Abdul-Rahman Majeed Al-Mansoor belched and patted prissily at his lips with a paper napkin.

Dorscht had a little silver box now which he evidently

kept with his crackers. He was selecting from it three kinds
of pills. One of them looked like valium.

Suddenly Forde sensed someone close to him, was aware
someone was staring at him. He turned his head and looked
up.

Her arm was raised as though she'd been about to touch
his shoulder.

"It *is*...isn't it?" she said.

"Yes."

He got to his feet.

"I'm so happy," she said.

"Karla," he said.

At the narrow end of the lake the water was shallow and
choked with weed. The air was rank with the smell of mud
and rotting vegetation. Karla stopped and pointed down
into the water.

"What is the name of this in English?"

Floating there just a foot from the edge of the lake was a
mass of frog spawn. He knelt on one knee and worked his
hands under the jelly, raising it slightly. It was the size of a
soccer ball. He was amazed at the weight of the mass,
amazed and then suddenly not amazed, pierced by memory,
transported back to his ten-year-old self. He saw himself
crouching beside a pool in an abandoned gravel pit which
was posted with signs saying DANGER. NO TRESPASS-
ING. On the ground beside him stood his big Ovaltine jar
with air holes punched through the lid. It was full of frog
spawn. He was catching palmated newts with a small net
made of clumsily-stitched lace curtain and placing them in
his weed-filled tin. All about him yellow coltsfoot flowers.

"In German," she said, "you say *Froschlaich.*"

Some of the intensely black dots were already starting to
elongate into commas. As she bent to look, her hair touched
his cheek. The mass of jelly poured out of his hands and
slipped back into the water sinking and then rising again to
ride just beneath the surface.

Forde felt almost giddy. His hands were tingling from
the coldness of the water. He felt obscurely excited by the

memory the feel of the frog spawn had prompted. He felt he could not breathe in deeply enough. The sun was hot on his back. After months of grinding winter it was a joy not to be wearing boots, a joy not to be wearing a parka, a joy to see the lime-green leaves, the froth of foliage, to hear bird song, sunlight hinting and glinting on the water, dandelions glowing, growing from crevices in the rock face the delicate fronds of hart's-tongue ferns.

He wanted to hold this place and moment in his mind forever.

Ahead of them a café bright with umbrellas. They sat at a patio table and drank cappuccinos, the lake's soft swell lapping at the patio's wooden pilings. Everything conspired to please, the sun, the water sounds, the stiffness of the foam on his coffee, the crisp paper wrapping on the sugar cubes. He watched her hands, the glint of transparent varnish on her fingernails.

Into a sudden silence, Forde said, "And...ah...Viktor?"

She raised an eyebrow.

"I suppose Viktor's with your husband."

"Oh, no," she said. "He's staying with a friend of mine from the university. He likes it there. She spoils him and she has a hound he can play with."

"Hmmm," said Forde.

"And he knows that when I return I will be bringing presents."

Forde nodded.

They walked on to finish the circuit of the lake. As they neared the hotel, Karla said, "Tell me about your name. I've often wondered about this. In English, people who are Robert are called Bob. So are you called Bob or Robert?"

"Well, sometimes Rob but the people closest to me seem to call me Forde."

She paused in the doorway.

"Then I, too," she declared, "will address you as Forde."

He sketched a comic caricature of a Germanic bow.

"My colleagues will be wondering where I am," she said. "I must go and hear a paper."

"We'll meet for dinner?"

She smiled and nodded.

"But I must change my shoes."

She put her hand on his arm and then turned and walked off across the hotel lobby.

He looked into the dining-room in hopes of finding Christopher but the buffet tables had been stacked away and a lone waiter was droning away with a vacuum cleaner.

Papers were being delivered in all the conference rooms. He eased open doors.

"...his fiction is sociolect and foregrounds the process of enunciation."

Christ!

"...the analytico-referential discourse reinstalls itself covering up a self-referential critique which...."

Christ!

In the small bar just off the lobby he settled himself with a bottle of Becks and, writing on the blank pages of an abandoned conference program, started to make notes. The feel of the frog spawn had unsettled him. He was startled by the intensity of the images and the spate of words he was dashing onto the pages. He had no idea what he might use it for, but he certainly wasn't going to question the gift.

Around the top of the old gravel pit bramble bushes grew in profusion. In late August and early September they were heavy with blackberries. He used the curved handle of a walking stick to draw the laden shoots toward him. He always took the blackberries to his grandmother who made blackberry and apple pies and blackberry vinegar to pour on pancakes.

His maternal grandparents lived in a tiny, jerry-built, company-owned row house not many miles from the pit where his grandfather had worked all his life. The backs of the houses looked onto a squalid cobbled square where vivid algae slimed the open drains. In the centre of the square stood a row of outhouses and a communal stand pipe. Surrounding the square were tumbledown sheds in which were kept gardening tools, work benches, rabbits, old bicycles, junk. And towering above the houses and the yard up on the hillside stood an abandoned factory.

The factory was a classic Victorian building of iron and glass. Had someone told him once it had been a shoe factory? Every time he had gone out of the back door, there it was, derelict, looming dark over the yard. Many of the glass panels were shattered or gaped blank. The road that ran up to the front of it was disused and closed off by an iron gate hung with threatening notices. Brambles and nettles grew right up to the walls. The building both lured and frightened him. It was a place of mystery. His mother and his grandparents had told him constantly of its danger.

"You go there," his grandfather cackled, "and the tramps'll get you."

Falling glass. Rotting boards. Trespass.

The pencil racing.

He bore in on it.

(Why machinery not melted down in 1939 for munitions?)

Inside—very quiet, *still*. The floor loud with glass. The light is dim—gloomy—subaqueous. Yes. Factory like sunken ship. Silt and weed have blunted its shape. The machinery is actually *changing shape*. What was once precise geometry—straight lines of steel—is now blurring, becoming *rounded* by rust and decay. Furred. Dali. Pigeon shit growing like guano. Whitewash on walls leprous and swollen. Brutality of the shapes and spaces oppressive. Girders, I-beams—name of place Nazis hanged Bomb Plot people with piano wire? Check. Spaces have that kind of feel.

What is going to happen here?

"There's Karla on the left," Forde said to Christopher.

They watched the three women coming across the lobby.

"Which do you think's the heavy?" said Christopher.

"What do you mean?"

"The minder."

"*What?*"

"Oh, really, Robert," said Christopher. "Don't be *impossibly* naive."

The other two women went into the dining-room.

"Karla," said Forde, "may I introduce you to Christopher Harris. Karla Schiff."

"Enchanted," said Christopher in a flat tone.

But the menu cheered him up. It was written in Slovene and English. It offered: Ham Dumplings with Fried Potatoes, Veal Ribs with Fried Potatoes, and Butter Pies with Chicken Pluck.

"That *is* rather good, isn't it?" said Christopher. "The Slovene would suggest they mean what Americans call 'Chicken Pot Pie.'"

The din was extraordinary and as wine bottles appeared was getting louder. Waiters and waitresses were carrying plates on the largest trays Forde had ever seen. They must have been four feet across. The waitresses were wearing what he thought of as Roman legionnaire sandals, straps wound up round the ankles and shin. Karla's shoes were made of plaited brown leather and were narrow and elegant and seemed to him very expensive-looking. He still felt slightly dissociated, still a little dazed by that world of memory and imagination, and was content to watch Karla and let rain down upon him the sparks and boom and brilliance of Christopher's performance.

Slovene wine production understandably collective rather than *Mis en Bouteilles au Château* so the height of praise would perhaps be the word *serviceable....*

Forde smiled and sipped.

Karla was wearing a loose white muslin blouse whose changing configurations kept his eye returning.

He wondered where Dorscht was seated; he sensed that Dorscht had immense possibilities.

He suddenly noticed that Christopher had tended to his nose with pancake makeup.

Frescos again. Mid-fourteenth century. The death of John the Baptist. A tiny perfect chapel near Bohinj. The headless corpse gouting blood in three streams. Angels decorated the other walls. One angel had a triple goitre.

"If only Bernard Berenson had visited Slovenia," Christopher said, "our frescos would be famous throughout the world."

"The Master of Bohinj," said Forde.

"The Master of the Goitre," said Christopher.

"Master of the Goitred Angel," said Forde.

"*Amico*," said Christopher, "of the Master of the Goitred Angel."

Forde laughed delightedly.

"It isn't kind, Forde," said Karla, "it isn't being nice to talk at dinner about things I don't understand."

Her lips moved into the faintest suggestion of a pout and Forde was enchanted.

As he sluiced his shirt in the washbasin, he burped and the taste of Tarragon Cake revisited him. They had gone to the bar off the lobby after dinner and had drunk something Christopher claimed was a local specialty, a pear brandy, but it hadn't tasted of pears and was aggressively nasty like grappa or marc and the bar had been cramped and jammed with people talking about the materiality of the signifier.

Forde was beginning to feel rather peculiar. He felt hot and somehow bloated though he had not eaten much of the ham dumplings. The fluorescent lights in the bathroom were unusually harsh and turned the white tiles, chrome and red rubber mat into a restraining room in a hospital for the criminally insane. He studied his face in the mirror. When he swallowed, his throat seemed constricted. He wondered if he was getting a cold.

He decided that he might ward it off by taking vitamin C and an extra aspirin. He took an aspirin every day to thin his blood. The heart attack that was going to fell him was never far from his conscious thought. He decided that if he took the vitamin C with a scotch from the mini-bar and added to the scotch a little *warm* water, this would render the scotch medicinal, but the drink burned and it felt as if he were pouring alcohol onto raw flesh. He had difficulty swallowing the pills.

He went back into the bathroom and took off his underpants to wash them and thought how very silly men looked naked but for socks. Pain was clutching his stomach. He sat on the toilet in the mad light emitting high-pitched

keening farts which culminated in an explosive discharge.
He stood and looked in the toilet and then bent and peered.
Finally, he knelt to look. Floating on the surface were three
whitish things each ringed with what looked like froth.
They looked exactly like the water-steeped jasmine flowers
in Chinese tea.

Florets, he thought.

An efflorescence in his bowels.

Benign?

Or cancerous?

Despite the aspirin, he still felt hot, feverish. He
switched on the bedside lamp. He lay naked on top of the
coverlet. The grey velvet on the walls was dappled with
faded spots which showed in this light like the subtle
rosettes on a black leopard's flanks.

He switched the light off and lay in the dark, feeling ill
and swallowing with difficulty. His head was aching. The
room felt close about him, furry. He seemed to sense the
grey walls almost imperceptibly moving as if they were
breathing. He slept fitfully, dozing, waking with a start,
drifting off deeper to lose himself in a chaotic and terrifying
dream, the narrow beam of his flashlight cutting into the
darkness, a trussed body hanging from a steel beam, the
broken glass loud under his feet.

On top of the cliff which rose at the head of the lake stood
another small castle. According to Christopher, it had been
extensively altered in the eighteenth century to turn it into
something more comfortable, more domestic. The Nazis
had used it as a recreation centre for army officers. Now it
had been turned into a museum which housed an absolutely
undistinguished collection of artifacts. Drinks and snacks
were served on the ramparts.

It was possible to climb up the cliff on a wandering trail
through the trees and then scramble the last 50 yards or so
on scree and skirt the parapet to come at a side gate.

Forde turned back and watched Karla scrambling up
below him. As she reached the steepest pitch, he leaned
down and extended his hand. She looked up at him,

winded, a smudge of hair stuck to her forehead with sweat. She reached up and grasped his hand and he took the weight of her and pulled her up over the last of the scree onto the track below the wall.

The museum delighted him. It was exactly like one-room museums in provincial English towns, haphazard accumulations of local finds, curios brought home by colonial officers, the last resting place of the hobbies of deceased gentry.

They browsed over the glass cases of unidentified pottery shards, stone hand axes, arrowheads, bronze fibulae, plaster casts of Roman and Greek coins, powder flasks of polished horn, bullet molds, bowls heaped with thirteenth-century coins of Béla IV of Hungary, fossils, Roman perfume bottles, stilettos, poniards, medieval tiles with slip decoration the colour of humbugs.

Forde stopped and exclaimed and bent over a display case.

"What is it?" said Karla.

"Look how pretty!" he said.

Forde stared at the leather object. He had never seen one before. The leather was rigid rather than pliable. It was a leather tube which flared like a champagne cork at the open end. Three quarters of the way up, the tube bent over like a cowl and tapered slightly to a close. The stitching was precise and delicate, the leather dark with age, glossy, and chased with a wreathing convolvulus design. The whole thing was about the size of a shuttlecock.

"It *has* to be," said Forde. "It's a hood for a falcon."

He was moved by the craftsmanship, by the thought of the hands that had gentled the hood over a hawk's head, by the sudden opening into the past the hood afforded.

"I'd love to touch that," he said. "I'd love to hold that in my hands."

He tried the case but it was locked.

When they'd exhausted the possibilities of the museum, they wandered out into the garden and then climbed to the ramparts and sat under an umbrella, sipping lemonade through straws. The length of the lake lay silver before them, the hotel, the marina, ex-King Peter's summer palace. A small yacht was tacking up toward them.

"You see, Karla," he suddenly burst out, "*that's* where art comes from. That leather hood. It arises from the realness of the world. Of course, art encompasses ideas but it's not *about* ideas. It's more concerned with feeling. And you capture the feeling through things, through particularity. There's nothing *intellectual* about novels."

Suddenly embarrassed, he busied himself with lemonade and straw.

Karla was reading his face.

They strolled back toward the hotel, following the road which led gently downhill all the way. Forde, still ravished by greenness, growth, the lemon-green of leaves, stopped to pick some wild flowers. He presented the bouquet to Karla. Daisies, white cow parsley, purple vetch, and campion both pink and white.

The venison was tough and fibrous. It was accompanied by a compote of red berries. Nobody knew what they were called but Professor Dorscht thought that in English they might possibly be called cloudberries. Though he could in no way guarantee that that was so.

Forde had been studying the program earlier and said to Dorscht, "So tomorrow's the day of your paper."

Dorscht inclined his head.

"About Lucy Maud Montgomery, isn't it?"

"Lucy *who?*" warbled Christopher.

"Specifically," said Dorscht, "the Emily novels."

"Emily?" repeated Forde.

"They are lesser-known works of her maturity."

Works, thought Forde, who considered it something of a national embarrassment that Canadian scholars and universities studied the output of a hack writer of children's books.

"This is another Canadian writer I do not know about it," said Karla. "There is so much for a Canadianist to learn."

"Oh, not really," said Forde who was tempted to express the opinion that the best of Canadian writing could be accommodated on a three-foot shelf.

Christopher was beginning to slur his words.

"Lucy *who*?" he said again investing the word "who" with patent incredulity.

"What I term the 'Emily' novels," said Dorscht, "is the trilogy of novels beginning in 1923 with *Emily of New Moon* and followed in 1925 by *Emily Climbs* and concluding in 1927 with *Emily's Quest*. My paper will—I think the most appropriate word is 'probe'—my paper will probe the trilogy's mythic aspects."

Mythic scrotums, thought Forde. *Mythic bollocks.*

Forde watched Dorscht peel his apple with a little silver penknife. His ability to digest was limited, he had explained, his health undermined by the tensions generated during the long years of study leading to his doctorate, years made unendurable by the psychological savagery visited upon him by his supervising professor.

"But what I mean *is*," insisted Christopher, "who *is* she?"

"*So*, Robert Forde!" boomed a familiar voice.

He automatically started to get to his feet, but a heavy hand on his shoulder rammed him down again into his seat.

"May I introduce," he said generally, "Drago Tomovic."

"And who," said Drago, "is this most *beauteous* lady?"

He smiled a gold-toothed smile that was revoltingly roguish.

"Drago has translated my novel *Winter Creatures* into Serbian."

Drago with mock flourish handed a package across the table. Forde tore open the paper.

It was in Cyrillic.

It had no cover art.

The paper was hairy.

Karla suggested they celebrate the translation in the bar off the lobby. The evening wore on. Drago's flappy jacket was in huge checks like the outrageous clothes worn by comedians in vaudeville or music hall. Christopher made it quite clear by grimace and the stiffness of his body that he found Drago appalling. Dorscht could not drink alcohol because of his ulcer. He also confided that he feared losing control. Drago flirted ponderously with Karla. Christopher started to read the translation making loud tut and click noises.

Through the surf of conversation Forde kept overhearing snatches of astounding drivel from a bony woman behind him who was, apparently, uncovering a female language by decoding patriarchal deformation.

Christ!

"Winter," boomed Drago, "is not just *winter*." He tapped his forehead. "*Think*! It *stands for* the coldness between the characters. Always say to yourself what is the *hidden* meaning of this book. Andrew is not *just* a bureaucrat. He works for the *government* and so *represents*...."

"You mean," said Karla, "that you read the book as...." She groped for the word. "...as an allegory?"

"*Certainly*," said Drago.

Forde was horrified.

"I make everything," said Drago, "*crystal clear*."

Dorscht went into another coughing fit.

When he'd finished and done the tic-thing with his left eye, Forde pressed him for details of the psychological savagery visited upon him by his supervising professor. Dorscht revealed that he had been commanded to write papers which his professor then appropriated and delivered at conferences as his own work. That the professor would only discuss his thesis in expensive restaurants where Dorscht was always forced to pay the bill. That for years he had to take the professor's clothes to the laundry and dry-cleaners and then deliver them to the man's house.

Christopher interrupted Dorscht's lamentations by slapping shut *Winter Creatures* and walking round the table to hand it to Forde, saying, "Oaf and boor."

To Dorscht, Karla and Drago, he said, "I am now going to bed."

His leaving broke the party up. Dorscht went off to take a valium and a mild barbiturate, Drago was swept up in the lobby by a noisy group of fellow Serbians who were all wearing what Forde took to be the rosettes and coloured favours of a soccer team, and Karla was claimed just outside the doors of the bar by her two friends from Jena.

She turned to look back at him; she smiled and shrugged.

Forde made his way up past the deer with blood in its nostrils, climbed the stairs at the pellet-pocked rabbit and the hawk with the shattered wing. His room felt stuffy and hot. He flipped through the translation of *Winter Creatures* but the only thing he could read was his name. But even if Drago had reduced a sprightly comedy to a stodgy allegory of his own invention, a book was still a book and it had his name on it. And if one thought of the Cyrillic as a kind of abstract art, the pages were not unattractive.

He filled the sink in the bathroom and poured in one of Sheila's Saran Wrap packages of Tide. He took off his clothes and immersed the shirt pushing it down repeatedly to get the air pockets out. He was beginning to feel decidedly odd again. A band of constriction across his forehead. Difficulty swallowing. He wondered if there were something about the room itself. Outside it, he felt entirely normal. Perhaps he was allergic to something in the room. Though he'd never suffered from allergies before. And the first night he'd slept in the room had been uneventful.

His mouth kept filling with saliva as if at any moment he might vomit. Perhaps they were using some devastating East European or Balkan chemical to clean the carpets or the bath.

He felt not only hot but distressed and confused by his discomfort. He wandered into the bedroom and sat in the armchair hoping that if he concentrated on reading he would be able to ignore or conquer the symptoms. He always travelled with a copy of *Hart's Rules for Compositors and Readers at the University Press Oxford* because it was small and inexhaustible. But the print swam and he kept putting the book down and staring at the furry wall, concentrating on not throwing up.

The venison?

But no-one else had seemed affected.

And didn't it take twelve hours or more to incubate or whatever one called it?

He forced himself back into the bathroom and scrubbed the shirt's collar and cuffs with the old toothbrush. He rinsed the shirt in the bathtub, leaving the soapy water in the basin to do his underpants and socks.

He sat on the toilet but nothing resulted. The fluorescent lights hummed. He thought suddenly of an eccentric landlady he'd once had when he was at university. She'd been having the house painted and had walked in on one of the painters who was on the toilet. In great embarrassment he'd said to her that he was having a pee.

"What kind of a man," she'd demanded, "sits down to squeeze his lemons?"

Why had *that* swum into his mind?

He lay on the bed and tried to sleep but under the covers he was too hot, on top of them too cold. The nausea had settled into uneasiness in his stomach and at the back of his throat. Pictures churned about in his mind. Karla looking up at him from the steep scree. The falcon's hood delicate and as light on the palm, he imagined, as a blown bird's egg. In the gilt cabinet, the plaited silk jesses with silver varvels. The roadside flowers. Pink and white campion.

He felt small cramps of pain in his stomach. He flung back the covers again and went to sit on the toilet. He strained briefly but nothing happened. He got up and realized immediately that something *had* happened. The toilet bowl was speckled with a fine mist of blood. Through the toilet paper his incredulous fingertips felt a lump, a lump with three—his fingertips explored that heat and hugeness—a vast lump with three.... What *was* this? A Pile? Piles? What *were* piles? Exactly? Such a thing had never happened to him before. His fingertips traced the dimensions and configurations of the horror. A lump with three...*lobes*.

The very word filled his mouth with clear saliva.

His hand smelled and was sticky with watery blood.

He twisted round trying to look at his behind in the mirror.

He put one foot on the toilet seat and bent forward separating his cheeks, but this position revealed nothing but redness.

A woman had once told him that after giving birth she'd had piles "like a bunch of grapes."

He waddled across the bedroom into the dressing-room with its full-length mirror and contorted himself variously and ingeniously but could see nothing. He imagined it to be blue or purple. He didn't want to get too yogic in his postures in case the horror burst.

He began to feel panicky. He could not endure the embarrassment of requesting treatment. But he did not wish to leak to death in a Slovenian hotel. He made a pad of a dozen or so Kleenex and wedged it between his cheeks and over the thing. He eased on clean underpants to keep the pad in place. Then he put on a clean shirt and his trousers and taking his key and the plastic ice-bucket set off down the corridor with tiny steps toward the ice machine.

Back in the bathroom he leaned his weary head on his arm on the vanity and with his right hand held ice cube after ice cube against the hot swollen lumps his body had extruded, ice water trickling down his legs into his toes, his scrotum frozen, fingers numb even through the flannel, weary, weary for his bed.

Forde was sitting with Karla. Christopher was sitting in the seat behind. The bus, one of four, was taking the conference people on this final day for a picnic in a village high up near Mt. Triglav in the Julian Alps.

Forde was feeling cheerful and restored. His piles had retreated entirely. His reading and lecture the day before had been well-attended. Even Forde had been surprised by how rude he had been to an earnest man at the lecture who had put a question to him which had involved the name "Bakhtin" and the words "dialogic," "foregrounded," and "problematized." Though he felt absolutely no contrition.

That night he had again felt ill and feverish but suffered nothing worse than a rash over his torso and thighs, hot white welts that itched and throbbed and bled when scratched. He had tried to soothe the itching by repeatedly applying a flannel soaked in ice-water.

He was sure he was suffering from an allergy either to something in the room or to food.

He had read from his last novel, *Tincture of Opium*. He'd done a restaurant scene involving the two lovers and a Chinese waiter who understood little English and whose every utterance sounded like a barked command. It was a set-piece but it performed well, modulating from near-farce to a delicate affirmation of love. He particularly liked the way he'd cut the sweetness of the sentiment with comic intrusions.

At dinner that night Karla had arranged with the Oliver Hardy waiter for a bottle of champagne to be brought to their table. She had proposed a toast to Forde's wonderful reading, to his glittering novels, to his eminence in Canadian letters, to his generosity with his time to beginning Canadianists, to, well, *Forde*!

She had been flushed, her eyes shining.

"Bottoms up!" cried Christopher.

"Sincere felicitations," said Professor Dorscht.

"To Forde!" said Karla again.

"*Certainly* to Forde!" boomed Drago.

Now he could feel her thigh swayed warm against his as the bus made turn after turn climbing the narrow road terraced into the mountain. The buses parked outside the boundary of the Triglav National Park, and people set out to walk the mile or so through woods and meadows to the village. The sun was pleasantly warm, the surrounding mountains serenely beautiful. The mountains enclosed them, cupped them. It was, thought Forde, rather like being on the stage of a vast amphitheatre. In places, the path they were walking along ran over outcroppings of rock. They stopped to help an elderly couple whose leather-soled shoes were slipping on the smoothed stone.

"What are those wooden things?" asked Forde.

"They're racks for drying hay on," said Christopher. "Unique to Slovenia. They're called *Kozolci*."

"And look!" said Forde. "Cowslips and primroses. I haven't seen those for years."

"And here," said Christopher, "are some of our famous

gentians."

Forde stopped. He stared down at the intensity of the blue.

"Oh, yes," said Karla. "In German we say *Enzian*."

"This is a very special day for me," said Forde. He got down on his knees and brushed the grass aside. "I've never seen a gentian before. I read about them when I was in my teens. I used to learn poems off by heart that I liked the sound of and there was one called 'Bavarian Gentians' by D.H. Lawrence. Well, perhaps it's not such a good poem. Perhaps you're extra forgiving to things you liked when you were young."

He looked up at Karla.

He frowned slightly in concentration.

Reach me a gentian, give me a torch!
let me guide myself with the blue, forked torch of this flower
down the darker and darker stairs, where blue is darkened on
    blueness
even where Persephone goes, just now, from the frosted
    September
to the sightless realm where darkness is awake upon the dark
and Persephone herself is but a voice
or a darkness invisible enfolded in the deeper dark
of the arms Plutonic, and pierced with the passion of dense
    gloom,
among the splendour of torches of darkness, shedding darkness
    on the lost bride and her groom.

"Stone the crows!" said Christopher. "Do you do that often?"

"No," said Forde. "It's weird. Only with things I learned when I was about sixteen."

"Sort of idiot savant-ish," said Christopher.

"It *sounds* beautiful," said Karla.

"Well," said Forde, getting up and brushing wisps of dry grass off his trousers, "sometimes I think its nothing *but* sound but then the old bastard gets off things like 'darkness is awake upon the dark' and you have to admit...."

The path through the meadow joined a wider path that led down into the village. A large banner was strung across the path. On it were the words:

WELCOME TO THE CULTURAL WORKERS

The straggling procession from the buses was beginning to pool now around the village hall where rustic tables and benches were set out. The villagers were greeting each newcomer with trays of bread and salt and shot glasses of slivovitz. The men were in Alpine costume, long tight white pants, thigh-high black leather boots, embroidered waistcoats. Cummerbund things. Or lederhosen. The women wore layered skirts and waistcoats and bonnets. Forde found it oddly unreal. Slightly embarrassing. He felt it was like being on the set of a Hollywood musical.

Some of the men were carrying crates of beer and cases of wine from the village hall and setting up one of the tables as a bar.

"The best beer," said Christopher, "is this Gambrinus. And Union's quite good, too. They brew that in Ljubljana. And for wine, I'd stick to Refosk or Kraski Teran."

"Who's paying for all this?"

"The Literary and Cultural Association of Slovenia and the local Party boss."

"And what about...."

"The peasants?" said Christopher.

"I wish you wouldn't keep saying that."

"Why?" said Christopher. "Peasants are a recognizable class. In France, Germany, Italy, Spain...*everywhere*. Peasants are peasants."

"Oh, *very* much in Austria and Bavaria," said Karla.

On the concrete slab in front of the village hall three young men were setting up amplifiers and speakers and going in and out of the hall trailing wire. Lying on and propped against the kitchen chairs were a bass, two guitars, and an amplified zither. Another man arrived and started messing about with a snare drum.

A little girl of about four or five dressed in skirts and bonnet was wandering through the tables staring at the people. She clutched to her chest an enormous and

48

uncomfortable-looking rabbit.

The drummer's peremptory rattings and tattings and paradiddles sounded through the roar of conversation. Two of the village women were spreading white linen tablecloths over three of the tables. As they flipped the cloths in the air, they flashed like white sails against the vast blueness, a sky so huge that it made him think of the word "empyrean." The warmth of the sun, the azure sky, the stillness of the mountains all around—a sigh of pleasure escaped him. Dishes, bowls, pans and platters began coming out of the village hall. They strolled over to look. Fried pork. Sausages with sauerkraut. Pork crackling. Fried veal with mushrooms. Pork hocks. Beans and chunks of veal in tomato sauce. Pasta stuffed with cottage cheese. Hunks of bread in baskets.

"That's the only thing to avoid," said Christopher, pointing. "It's a sort of cheese pie called *Burek* and it's *terminally* greasy."

They filled paper plates and Christopher exchanged pleasantries with the man behind the bar and snagged a bottle of Refosk.

The band started to play polkas and waltzes. An accordion came to join them. The music was just the thing for a picnic in the Alps, jolly and silly. Forde drank more wine and found himself tapping his foot in time to the rattletrap drummer.

He noticed some of the village men raising their hats to a man who had just arrived. He was wearing a black suit and a black shirt with a priest's white collar. But on his head was a bowler hat with pheasant feathers pinned to one side of it to form a tall, swaying cockade. He made his way through the villagers, shaking hands and slapping backs until he reached the bar where he was immediately handed not a shot glass but a tumbler of slivovitz. Forde had known some gargantuan drinkers in his day but he had never before seen a man *purple* with drink.

"He is both notorious and widely loved," said Christopher. "Later on—he always does—he'll sing a selection of sentimental and dirty songs."

When they'd finished eating, Forde volunteered to fetch beer. The slow beer line-up brought him alongside a table of cultural workers who, seemingly oblivious to meadows or mountains, were locked in earnest discussion. As he stood there he heard a man say "univocal discourse." He looked with loathing upon these moneychangers in the temple.

As he put the three bottles of Gambrinus down on the table, Christopher was saying, "Well the high point of the day for me is the absence of that hulking *Serb*."

"Drago is not my fault," said Forde.

"He certainly isn't mine."

"Certainly!" said Forde. *"Certainly!"*

The crowd around the food tables was thinning out. Some of the conference people had drifted away higher in the meadow and were lying down sunbathing. The band had returned after a break and was playing waltzes. Forde had had enough to drink for the day to feel dreamlike and desultory. Some couples were waltzing in the village street. Forde idly watched the swirl of skirts. The sun was getting hotter. He started to peel the label off his beer bottle.

Karla got up and, pointing down the street, said, "Forde! Take me dancing."

He looked up at her.

He hesitated.

"Karla," he said. "I have eaten sausage and sauerkraut. Fried potatoes. Fried mushrooms. And that sheep cheese. I must have drunk a bottle of wine. And beer. I *might*," he said, "just might be able to manage a slow stroll in the meadows."

People started to crowd around the band.

"Must be Father Baraga," said Christopher.

They walked over and joined the crowd. Father Baraga was sitting on a wooden kitchen chair, hands on his thighs, beaming and purple. The zither man was lowering and adjusting the microphone. The musicians conferred with Father Baraga and a song was agreed upon.

It was obviously a kind of patter song, and the priest accompanied it with exaggerated facial expressions indicative of leering surprise, outrage, shock. Everyone who understood Slovene was laughing and grinning.

"What's it about?"

"Oh, this is a mild one," said Christopher. "It's all innu-endo and *double entendre*. Like old music hall songs." He thought for a second. "You know,

'In the spring, my Auntie Nellie,
Dusting down her Botticelli'

that sort of thing."

Watching the rubbery lips, the sweat running from the bags under his eyes, the spittle, the purple flesh bulging onto the white collar, the yellow stumps of his teeth, Forde felt again how dreamlike, even nightmarish, the world so often seemed.

His novels were often criticized for containing what re-viewers and critics described as "grotesques" and "carica-tures." What world, he wondered, did they live in? They carped and belly-ached that some of his scenes were "im-probable" or "strained credulity" yet Forde knew that this was the way the world *was*. The world was bizarre. The word "normal" was simply a notion.

He shrugged as he thought about it.

He was more than half-way up a very high mountain lis-tening to a fender bass being played by a man in thigh-length leather boots, to two guitars being played by men in lederhosen, to an amplified zither being played by another man in thigh-length leather boots, and to the singing of a drunken Roman Catholic priest wearing a bowler hat with feathers in it. *And* he was in the company of a woman Christopher had implied might well be a Stasi informer.

Karla caught his eye and motioned with her head. He followed her, working his way out of the crowd. They strolled up through the meadow, past the sunbathers, past hay racks, until they were high enough on the narrow trail to look down on the roof of the village hall. Karla was wearing her hair in a ponytail that bobbed as she walked. He thought of the photograph she'd sent. The photograph that was inside the calendar in his desk drawer. In that pic-ture her hair had been short and helmet-shaped.

They could see only three houses on the main street with

another set back from it by about 50 yards. Not that the street was really a street. It was just an unpaved, sandy path. The rest of the houses were dotted about the meadows. As they stood there, Forde was very aware of Karla's toenails. She had painted them a silvery colour.

The path they were walking along ran in front of three houses, grouped together. The house in the centre sported a frieze of stylized flowers painted just below the eaves. Outside the house stood the little girl in skirts and bonnet they'd seen earlier lugging her rabbit about.

The rabbit was lying in the grass unmoving except for one ear which turned to monitor its world. Karla smiled at the child and bent down to pet the rabbit.

"Das ist doch ein hübscher Kerl!"

The child laughed and swooped on the rabbit, hauling it up to her chest, its hind legs dangling. Just as Karla reached out to stroke it, the rabbit squirmed and raked the inside of her forearm with its back legs. She cried out in surprise. The little girl dropped the rabbit and squatted beside it and seemed to be scolding it. As Forde watched, blood welled into the two scratches, rose into large beads, ran.

"Animal things are always bad news," said Forde. "Dog bites, that sort of thing. They're always dirty. You probably ought to get a tetanus shot, but for now...."

He took her arm. He held her with his left hand just above her elbow. With his right hand he held her hand. He bent over the inside of her forearm. On her wrist he could smell the fragrance of *Ysatis*. He sucked the length of the two scratches, filling his mouth with blood and spitting it out onto the grass. Suck and spit. Suck and spit.

Karla laced her fingers with his.

His mouth tasted vile and he could hardly get his eyes open. He'd obviously slept for far longer than the nap he'd intended. His watch had stopped. He went into the bathroom and looked at his puffy face in the mad fluorescence. He'd caught the sun.

He went down to the dining-room. The lobby was

deserted. He heaved open the door to the dining-room. The vast room was empty and silent. The chandeliers blazed light on the emptiness. By the trestle tables used as a service station, two of the waiters were silently folding a tablecloth. Arms raised above their heads, the corners of the cloth held between thumb and forefinger, they advanced upon each other. The corners met. The fat waiter stooped and picked up the bottom edge. He retreated until the cloth was taut then advanced again to meet and make a second fold. They looked as if they were performing an elephantine parody of a courtly dance.

The door thunked shut behind him.

He went into the bar off the lobby. There were three people there. He supposed some of the conference people had already left. He discovered that it was nearly 9.30. The buses had arrived back at Splad at about 6.30 so he'd been asleep for nearly three hours. He wound his watch and reset it.

He wondered if he ought to call Karla or Christopher.

He stood in the silent lobby in indecision.

Then he turned and started up the stairs, left at the deer, up the stone steps at the rabbit and hawk, hardly noticing them now they were familiar. He felt quite groggy from the unexpectedly deep sleep. He sat in the armchair in the bedroom and immediately started to feel even worse. His mouth was filling with saliva. He was feeling waves of nausea. He mastered the surge of vomit long enough to get into the bathroom where he vomited copiously and uncontrollably. He braced himself with both hands against the wall and stood, head hanging over the toilet bowl, breathing through open mouth, drooling, strings of saliva and mucus glistening from his lower lip. His stomach seized again and again and he vomited until he was vomiting nothing but bile and his throat was raw. He was in a cold sweat and his legs were trembling. He could feel the sweat cold on his ribs.

When the nausea faded, he brushed his teeth and cleaned the rim of the toilet and the underside of the spattered toilet seat. As he was doing so, he realized that something was happening to his vision. Bright white sparks seemed to be drifting across things, the sensation intensifying until there was a gauze obscuring things like the snow of interference on a TV screen. He felt quite frightened and went back into the bedroom feeling his way along the walls. He got himself onto the bed and lay there wondering what was happening to him, what he ought to do.

He opened his eyes again, but the silent crackle of white dots still veiled the bedside lamp, the occasional table, the bed itself. He closed his eyes and tried to think calmly about his situation. Were the vomiting and the white dots related? Could they have the same cause? Why might he have vomited? Wine? Extremely unlikely. Might he be suffering from sunstroke? Might the white dots be a migraine headache? Though he'd never had one before and his head wasn't aching.

He lay on the bed and tried to relax. He breathed as slowly as he could, trying to slow the rate of his heartbeat. Despite his anxiety and the churning questions and formulations in his mind, his head turned into the pillow and he drifted some of the way toward sleep.

And on the threshold of sleep, he sees himself walking along a hospital corridor. As he passes each open doorway, the sudden warm smells of sickness. He is standing near a bank of elevators looking out of the window onto the flat, gravelled roof. The roof is mobbed with pigeons and seagulls screeching and squawking and fighting for the scraps thrown out of windows by patients and orderlies. The roof is seething with the bodies of birds. They tread upon each other. Pigeons are pecking cigarette butts and a dead pigeon. The gulls are threatening each other, pumping up raucous challenges. One rises to a piercing crescendo only for another to start over again. The screeching of the gulls heard through the glass merges with geriatric wailing further up the corridor, a cacophony of aggression, fear and despair.

He goes into the room. It has two beds in it but only one is occupied. The nurse is bent over the person in the bed. The sheets and blankets are pulled back off the bed and trail on the floor. The nurse plaps a sanitary napkin onto the polished linoleum. It is bloody. She withdraws a syringe and caps it and puts it on a stainless-steel tray on the bedside table.

He goes around the bed and looks down at Sheila. Her eyes are closed. He puts his hand on her arm. It is cold and clammy. Karla is wearing a stethoscope. She looks up at him across the bed.

She shakes her head.

The room is silent. The only sound other than Sheila's rapid, shallow breathing is the screeching of birds.

The bus that had been laid on for Ljubljana pulled out of the hotel car park onto the road that led to the highway. There were a dozen or so passengers from the conference, none that he'd spoken to before. He was returning to the Holiday Inn.

He'd woken only half an hour earlier and in a panic to catch the bus he'd foregone a shower, stuffed his possessions into his bag, paid the mini-bar bill at Reception, gulped down a tepid black coffee standing in the bar off the lobby.

The bus had been his only chance of getting into Ljubljana in time. He had agreed to give a lecture that afternoon at the University of Ljubljana; yet another honorarium had been mentioned.

A few introductory... the professor had said...*and such and so.*

He gazed out of the window. His stomach was empty and rumbling and he still felt flustered from rushing about but at least he could *see*. The screen of white dots had disappeared entirely. He had Christopher's address in Sweden and he would write to him—and to Karla—to explain his disappearance the night before and his unceremonious departure.

The journey took just over an hour. The room that had been reserved for him was actually vacant and ready for occupation. He poured a package of Tide into the washbasin and washed the shirt he'd been too ill to deal with the night before. His flight the next day to Frankfurt left at eight in the morning. The trip to the airport took some twenty minutes to half an hour. He liked to be early so he would need a taxi at six-thirty. The hotel could doubtless supply one, but he had accepted a business card from the driver who had driven him in from the airport and had promised to phone him. He suspected the man was desperate for the business. The switchboard got him the number and eventually he made himself understood and completed the arrangements.

He went downstairs and ate breakfast in the Holiday Inn restaurant in solitary state. Four unenthusiastic waiters stood about. He worked his way through a mushroom omelette and three rolls with butter and plum jam and felt soothed and restored after the purging his stomach had suffered in the night. The morning fog was dispersing, the sun burning through. He decided that he would go for a walk along the Ljubljanica River and then devote the rest of the morning to finding presents for Sheila, Chris and Tony. As he strolled out into the plaza in front of the hotel, he was feeling a lightness of spirit, almost a jauntiness.

Presents for Chris and Tony would prove far more difficult than finding a present for Sheila. They seemed to be interested only in rock bands, basketball and strange fantasy magazines involving dragons, mazes, dungeons and monsters. Pleasant enough boys but he found them rather blank. Sheila said they'd turn out just fine, that all boys were like this. What he was seeing was just adolescent conformity. Beneath were two sturdy individuals. Forde trusted Sheila's understanding of people and did not doubt that she was right. What troubled him was what they didn't *know*. Things like History and Geography. Sheila had told him he was becoming cranky.

Two years previously he'd taken the pair of them to England to visit their grandparents. He had shown them Buckingham Palace, the Tower of London, the British Museum, Westminster Abbey, all the delights of London. He had taken them to Warwick Castle. To Stratford to see Shakespeare's birthplace. To Oxford. Through the Cotswold villages. Chris had been—he thought for a moment—

eleven and Tony thirteen.

He had tried to give them a sense of the past, to connect them with it. He'd pointed out tumuli in the fields and medieval strips and baulks still visible under the turf. He had taken them through an iron-age hill fort. He'd marched them along The Ridgeway from the White Horse at Uffington to the megalithic long barrow called Wayland's Smithy, rhapsodizing the while that their feet were treading the same ground that tribes and armies had marched on since prehistory.

On their return to Canada, Chris had confided in Sheila that the place he'd liked most, the very best place they'd visited, was Fortnum and Mason. The high point of the expedition for Tony, apparently, had been the purchase of an extra-large T-shirt on the Charing Cross Road, a T-shirt bought without consultation, on which was printed front and back: Too Drunk To Fuck.

It was in the bookstore where he'd seen in the window the omnibus edition of Jalna novels by Mazo de la Roche that he happened upon the perfect gift for Sheila. The book was a facsimile edition in superb colour of a famous medieval Jewish book in the collection of the National Museum in Sarajevo. The book was in a slipcase which also contained a pamphlet in English detailing the book's history.

It was known now as the *Sarajevo Haggadah*. One hundred and forty-two vellum pages. The text was illuminated lavishly, initial words in gold and a blue so intense it might have been made with powdered lapis lazuli. Hebrew characters became flowers; heraldic and fanciful beasts stalked the intricate foliage. Just as beautiful was the chaste unadorned calligraphy of the prayers. The stories of the Exodus were illustrated with nearly a hundred miniature paintings.

The *Sarajevo Haggadah* was thought to have been written and painted most probably in Barcelona shortly after 1350. When the Jews were expelled from Spain in 1492, the book had started its journey eastward. There was a record of it in Italy in 1609. It was carried into the Balkans, most probably to Split or Dubrovnik by a family called Kohen. The book was sold to the National Museum in Sarajevo in 1894.

He was touched that reproduced on some pages were the spots and blotches from wine and food spilled on the book during Seders over the centuries. And it pleased him to think that next Passover when they went to Toronto for the Seder, Sheila would be able to read along in something more sumptuous than the prayer books her father handed out and her father would be able to pontificate on the historical prohibition against art in sacred texts in the Jewish tradition and when he discovered the book was Sephardic he would launch into rambling assaults on Ladino as a language and the eccentricity, if not impurity, of Sephardic rites and Sheila's mother would either contradict him or introduce a new topic of conversation she'd derived from TV talk shows such as the spontaneous combustion of human beings and within minutes everyone would be shouting and on it would go, on and on it would go....

At 6.30 he was waiting in the lobby with his carry-on bag, his briefcase, and his furled umbrella. The night had passed restfully and without incident. He had not bothered with breakfast as it would be served on the plane and he'd be able to get coffee at the airport. He was brooding about his carry-on bag. Because he was up early, the collar and cuffs of his shirt were still slightly damp and clammy. He had worn the same shirt every day except for the day before when migraine or whatever it had been had prevented his washing it. But it was obvious that, normal circumstances prevailing, one shirt would suffice. If he were to cut out seconds on socks and underpants as well, it might be possible to get essentials into a briefcase alone. He stood looking out of the plate glass window. It was slightly foggy again. Not enough to delay take-off, he hoped. Checked his watch. He thought it would be something of a triumph if he could dispense with a carry-on bag, if he could get into his briefcase alone any necessary papers and the essentials—toothbrush, toothpaste, hairbrush, *Hart's Rules*, razor, cellophane twists of Tide, aspirins. Light glowed on the fog. The taxi turned into the plaza and drew up under the porte-cochère.

The driver greeted him warmly and they shook hands. As they cleared Ljubljana itself, the fog seemed to be thinning. They'd been driving along for about fifteen minutes when the car slowed and the driver signalled a left turn. Forde listened to the click-click-click of the indicator. The driver turned off the main road and into a narrow side road.

"Is this the way to the airport?" said Forde.

The driver raised his forefinger and nodded, a gesture obviously meaning: Just be patient. Wait for a minute. At the bottom of the hill, the driver pulled up onto the grass verge. Forde felt slightly apprehensive. He hoped he wasn't being set up. He looked at his watch. They got out and Forde followed the driver along the road until they came to a stone bridge. The driver put his finger to his lips and then gestured for Forde to stoop. They approached the centre of the bridge bent almost double and then rose slowly to peer over the side.

The river was quite wide and mist hung over it. In the middle of the river was a long narrow island. Standing at the near end of the island were two cranes and some little distance behind them a nest, a great platform of gathered sedge and reeds.

The cranes were bowing to each other, their heads coming down close to the ground. One of the birds fanned out its bustle of tail plumes and started to strut circles around the other, every now and then leaning in toward it sideways as if to gather or impart intimacies. Then the crane with the raised plumes walked over to the messy nest and began to parade around it, pausing from time to time to bow deeply toward it.

The other bird raised its great wings over its back and jumped into the air. The other responded by launching itself sideways, a collapsing, hopping jump. The jumps looked like the hopeless efforts of a flightless bird to take wing. They started jumping together. There was something comic in the spectacle. It was as if these huge and stately birds were being deliberately juvenile and ungainly. The way they trailed their legs suggested the way dancers in musicals jump and click their heels together in the air. Their antics were oddly incongruous. The birds were so regal, so dignified that to see them flap and hop and topple was as if two portly prelates in gaiters suddenly started to caper and prance.

One of them stretched its long heron-like neck straight up into the air and gave forth a great trumpet blast of noise, harsh and unbelievably loud.

Krraaa-krro.

The other bird straightened the S of its neck and replied.

Krraaa-krro.

And then the two birds paced toward each other until their breasts were touching and began to rub each other's necks with their heads, long swooping and rising caresses, their beaks nuzzling at the height of the embrace.

The driver took out a packet of cigarettes and lit one. Forde realized that his fingers were clenched over the edge of the stone block. The smell of tobacco hung on the air.

The driver grinned at Forde.

Forde smiled back.

The cranes trumpeted at the sky, first one then the fierce reply, reverberating blasts of noise bouncing off the stonework of the bridge filling the air with the clamour of jubilation.

Forde felt....

Forde exulted with them.

California Cancer Journeys

Mark Anthony Jarman

I dwindle...dynamite no more.
I ask for a natural death,
no teeth on the ground—Robert Lowell.

At sea, a whitewater ferry crossing, rocking our way to Port
Angeles on the venerable M.V. Coho. The Customs man
on the other side looks like my dead father. He drawls an
order: "You bring us back some sunshine now."

We drive verdant Highway 101 for a day before sneaking up on Interstate 5 and its oceanless rain and speed
blurring county after sandy county. Five heads, five brains,
$500 in traveller's cheques: my brand new family entering
that ordered thirteen-day hallucination that is the trip to
Grandmother's house. Grandmother, Sharon's mother,
possesses any number of amiable cancers. We want to visit.
She is looking forward to our visit. Our job is to bring
sunshine.

At the same moment, in an upstairs room of a half-finished
farmhouse in Grande Prairie, my best friend Levi is trying
to kill a brain tumour; perhaps this fabled presence in his
skull looks like a softball, or perhaps an orchard tangle.
Whatever: Levi has lost interest in metaphor. He's taking
injections in the thigh. He shuns chemo. He travels to
Hawaii instead. R & R. While we travel, Mr. Levi Dronyk's
brain is on a parallel journey. We move and something in
his head moves, shakes out tiny reticulate leaves. They cut
out as much tumour as they could without making him a

61

vegetable (My vegetable love should grow more slow). They couldn't yank all its tendrils without cutting his brain. Standing in my sunlit backyard Levi talks to me, he's still himself. He's lost some vocabulary but he's still Levi. How long will this last? The doctors don't like to tell you you're dead. They want you to obey them. Balance and release seems the name of this relentless new dream, disease the new Elizabethan masque.

A first trip for our children; Gabriel is six months, Kelly is two years, and Martin is four. They love dinosaurs and bloodthirsty pirates. They love their parents. We gaze out clear car windows; we take in America the beautiful while something hesitant tries to shut down in my friend's head. Eighteen years I have known Levi. Windows close, a humming human ailment creeping in a joyful conspiracy, an impractical joke blossoming with the same crazy energy he displayed in everything: softball, beat poetry, chicken-skin music, union business, random city travel, wild letters and dubbed tapes mailed to friends in the mountains. Levi wanted us to know the new singers, the obscure voices with their implied eyes and lipsync violence, their homey versions of winter. Selling his share of the house and blowing the money on records. Levi plays with his one-year-old by my garage. I think, His children will not know him. His records will last longer. He has no estate. He wanted to play a shining horn, had the Motown moves down like stink; a good dancer, a sharp-dressed man with a hawk-like Slavic face, a good talker and romancer. Now Levi will be the guy that died years ago. The guy that stood squinting by my garage with his one-year-old. He'll be the guy that worked for the union, giving twenty years to a small TV station, to phantom voices and talk shows and electric lines zipping right through his head all day everyday. Levi got zapped, he got a smoked brain as a dowry, a perk from the owners, like a poached smokehouse salmon. Inhaling the room, fuming, fusing, having the company air while having an affair with the woman at work: and then someone slashed the roof of his Mustang in the staff lot, the car he had to sell later, bankrupt, moving from town to town, prowling the boondocks of affordable real estate. Who orders a life wisely?

We try. Sharon and I have borrowed against the house and bought a new car, a white car from a country both our fathers fought against. We drive under the huge hydro towers, following the ordered lines of the American Aqueduct, the orchards, this translation of the banquet with bouquets, this demon demonstration of the demand for water, the inalienable right to take over. Los Angeles is thirsty for power, lights, action. California Republic is thirsty; its lines run off the globe, its big metal legs stride the world, a Colossus, a shaking tectonic hangover. As I drive staring at the wires that lead off the horizon, I wonder, Could you actually *run* atop this power line tightrope, run all the way to some East L.A. taco stand? Walk a wire to that lovely infestation of poseurs and confidence men and executive producers? Would it kill you if you're not careful, not articulate? Could you walk to Los Angeles' Crip frijoles or would it fry your brain first? Not unlike TV screens and TV monitors and wires raving all around you in a tiny editing-room.

At work Levi was surfing electrical waves, moving his waged brain through a web of invisible beams and hemlines, through bones and border crossings. We force our new car to leap through invisible interstate borders; my three young kids dazed, thirsty, their new blond heads swivelling, leaving home for the first time, miles to go before we weep. New miles go on the new car. That's all right: rack them up, rack up the miles.

At the other end of these thick wires they are jump-starting a tiny star in the concrete sidewalk, fixing a hole where the rain got in, where they worship the saucers and strangle hookers with their own bra. The quake drops sections of freeway. Hop-scotch. It's exciting to arrive at midnight, as if party to a moonlight escape.

Trying to remember the motive, the votive, the fine print, we go through the spiny and naked desert, through the non-woods to Grandmother's house. Breast cancer was her first wolf; bone cancer was next. Her hip. Then her ribs. At least it's not soft tissue. Soft tissue is without hope. Maybe she'll escape. The social contract has changed since our last visit. Now one brings a basket of shark cartilage, cranberry juice, hoping and making small talk: My what big teeth. Yes well you know they're all using teeth whitener now, like Tom Cruise.

Oh is that so? one says.

Yes. He's into some cult. They all have personality problems. They have a distorted view of life.

But very distorted is what sells, very distorted is boffo box office.

Yes, that's true enough, I say. This is a nice house you have here, I say.

Hmmph. More like half a house, Gladys complains. (It's bigger than our place and she lives alone.) She painted over the "yella," transplanted small palm trees, she owns it outright, but it's not really her place. She's magic with succulents, blossoms, fruit trees. The avenues are lined with gold and guacamole, but she's depressed about everything.

"I just don't know what's going to come of this," she says. "I don't know what's at the other end of this now." She's from the treed hills of Pennsylvania. No-one here is like her and she's alone most of the year. The barrios are too close. Her oldest daughter, Sharon's big sister, died of a brain tumour. She died when Nixon was President. Her parents voted for George Wallace. I had never before met anyone who voted for Wallace.

"I'm in pretty bad shape. Where's the baby? How did this happen," she wonders. Mexican workers outside listen to a Spanish version of Blondie's *Call Me*. They drive in, work fast on the perfect grass, and get out. Diagonal stripes. The teenage Italian woman across the street bleaches her hair white as cocaine and favours leopardskin and leather. Everyone strives to be blonde, to be dark, to be hip, to be ethnic, to be straight, to be crooked, to be something they saw in *Interview* magazine. No-one here votes for George Wallace. The pavement glitters. They've never heard of George Wallace. It's a house of straw in a storm, a stop, likely her last in this state. Neighbours pretend no-one else exists, avert their eyes when I try to say hi. Dying is not the in thing. Unless you're beautiful and famous. And how long will she exist? Can she escape this? Gladys has stopped going to the movies or walking at night. Gladys has stopped playing pipe-organ at the church. Soon she'll have to stop driving. Then the rented wheelchair: I can't get to the bathroom at night! Then: I can't get out of bed, I'm choking because I have to eat on my back. I have no garden; I'm going to drown in a teaspoon. This, you recall, is California. There is always that struggle to keep mobile, to unlearn the unclean past: The frightening sun of a polished asylum, the sum of every plane alive and reflecting its new sheen. Doubt not, though no-one will buy an older house, an old shoe or an old story unfolding under an old sun squeezing out too much light over the new house up the cul-de-sac from the giant power lines, the new house in the 24 hour white sun with grass green as paint and grieved with envy beside the spare brittle music of the desert.

In the back of my head I keep hearing the Sons of the Pioneers croon, "Water, cooool clear water." And perhaps this is how tumours begin: something as innocent as an irritating song; that piece of sand that leads to the pearl that leads to the heebie jeebies or the mulberry bush or the river worth gathering at. No-one lied to us: the wind rides in from the foggy salt ocean and splits in the scorched valley; the wind heads south and the wind heads north, riding madly in all directions at once. Sea and desert; here are spirited worlds meeting and stripping each other like sex. Birds panic in their guided skyway. Ladders grow into the leather trees, searching for what grows. Like a tumour in a good friend's head. A double helix ladder. The pickers used to be Chinese. They had to go.

Hikers find smashed earthenware in a cavern, broken crockery in a head. Anarchy in a tiny place. Or is sickness a normal state, and health unnatural? Someone slashed the roof of Levi's Mustang; the surgeon slashed the roof of Levi's haunted head.

My quiet father died last year in California on Valentine's Day. He had a heart attack while walking out for a copy of *The San Diego Union*. He made it back to the rented condo but my mother was at the pool above the sandy cliffs, waiting for him. Finally she knew she had to check. She told me later I was lucky not to hear the sounds he made on someone else's chesterfield. They lost him at the hospital. I'm beginning to associate California with death, with sounds I should not hear. He had been diagnosed with liver cancer but the heart stepped up first. The squeaky wheel gets the grease, greases *you*. People said we were lucky not to see him waste away. To nothing. My aunt in England wrote me: "One felt he was the sort of chap who would go on forever quite cheerfully. As in life he was considerate to the end and to me it seems he decided to unfold his wings and just fly away—thoughtful as ever." At the Coroner's he lay in the sliding drawer. My mother kissed him goodbye for all of us.

On the highway we read air's long history, the grasses waiting to bend, willing to wilt, while cattle hang on steep hillsides with black stoic faces; and the white horse lingers, looking for just one tree's shelter. I don't know if my father flew away. The pressed grasses are written on, something in this country stolen or moved and something genuine and fine. The greasers stare at the ground, at the creosote, at the white horse. The Sons of the Pioneers keep singing of water, singing of cool water.

This is my three sons' first long trip. They seem so well behaved, benign (as opposed to malignant). We fall from motel beds and drive about three inches and Martin asks if we're looking for a motel yet.

Soon, I say, in about twelve hours.

Why? he asks. How come? How long is twelve hours?
I don't know.

He'll forget it after a while. I've forgotten so much. Like reservations. I walk into motel offices covered in baby spit-up and cranberry juice and demand a business discount. I'm in the business of raising blond kids; I'm in the business of going through the non-woods to or from Grandmother's house. I want my discount.

Take Jesus into your heart, they say. Take Jesus into your liver, they don't say. When they're older and my graphic heart or liver has burst will my children remember this earthquake country? This voodoo volcano country? The squashed valleys with such a hard light that all the year's colours have gone dull? Will my young wife become pregnant at my wake? Believe me: I know of this exact event. Remember me, mumbles the ghost bent under the stage in a leather jerkin. Ah forget it, he says after a while.

There is no shade, no cover, just saltwhite ground and greasewood scrub, rattlesnakes and Borax muletrain memories. Will my children remember falling between the motel bed and motel wall and screaming, trapped, not knowing where they are? I tried to soothe them. This stripped mezzotint country reminds me of Merle Haggard and the Strangers; Buck Owens and the Buckaroos. These clouds have never seen clover. I remember bits of these trips with my parents. The patched canvas tent and the moose bellowing in the river. The Lethe Motel & Bar-B-Q. The bobcats jumping on tourists and the backseat's play within the play. Will our children remember *us*? We know so little of where we pass: last week, last decade, last century. Think of the pobladores, the lost families in this series of valleys: Alvarado, Castro, Wolfskill, Pico, Duran, Pacifico, de la Guerra y Noriega. The irrigation squabbles, scalps lifted like weeds, night riders and vigilante lynchings, complicated slaughter in the blind canyon. Now: brief moon-flowers and insects and cement overpasses with cratered pale masses of swallow nests glued to their side, cells mutating like you know what. Waiting for the airport and the surveyors' ribbons and subdivisions and the all-night Mexican places. We see no people, see no rabble. Just the power lines; just the huge Möbius road. What used to seem an *escape.*

Who lives here other than kingsnakes and sidewinders and swallows and their aboriginal oatmeal nests? Where are they all hiding? The dusty questions as you roll blind and yawning through another squinting crossroads, rattle your fine city bones on another corduroy road, past adobe bungalows and hedge-rows that have run out of talent.

Sharon says, "My mother is dying and she still has that ability to drive me crazy." Gladys sprays more chemicals at the spiders in her garage, eats fast food from Jack-In-The-Box. She points to the pastel houses: This is what we call a development. Will she be resurrected again? Or is this the last time? It's the last time. It's a development. She has been gathering in death for a decade, learning and turning dying into performance art. I do the dishes every night at 7.20. I am restless, spooked. My children are thrilled by this trip to see their dying grandmother. They bang and clang on her piano and break her sprinkler system and scatter rocks to meet the Mexican's lawnmower. At night, though, my children cry out from their sleeping-bags on the floor, afraid of her Victorian furniture piled high in their room. Their grandfather (divorced and remarried) flies in from Las Vegas to tell war stories, stories I like more than anyone. He apologizes for telling them, apologizes for the divorce.

Gladys' lungs slowly fill with fluid; there is a hole in her hipbone from radiation. She shuffles into the kitchen, zaps her frozen "entrée."

"There is a level," she says, "beyond which I won't allow myself to fall." That doesn't last long. That level is history. History is a bunkbed. Her ribs start killing her. Her doctor quits and the office is bedlam. After a fortnight of sunny chaos we have lost our heads, lost our sleep, lost our saintly intentions; Sharon and I just want to get the hell out, to escape California Republic, to stop drinking cranberry juice. Gladys wants to die and she cannot; she lives on, mourning doves mumbling from her steep backyard. She hallucinates, believes she is chasing chickens in Pennsylvania, is shopping for bargains at the mall, that she is going to have to sue. Levi wants to live and yet he dies. The message arrives from Grande Prairie thousands of miles to the north: He's dying, she says, he's checking out. News falls from the buzzing wire, Levi falls from the wire without learning the instrument. Mourning doves have such slim heads. This end has happened so fast I can't believe it. As students Levi and I hopped the ferry to Port Angeles to drink in The Salty Dawg, to thumb up to the glacier at Hurricane Ridge. Suddenly someone is coming to get my friend Levi in a pickup truck, crossing the northern steppes to pick up what's left of him, as if he is a bale of green hay or a dry cord of tamarack to be burned. Not even a purple hearse to Joshua Tree. Not even a drummer or a staggering New Orleans horn.

How to forget that urge to escape somehow? And escape exactly what? Escaping escape? The restless dishes at 7.20? The salt on the ground? The routine blossoms inside your skin and skull? The desert sand that should look different on Valentine's Day? Or is it the displays in all the Encinitas shop windows: those red shiny Valentine hearts everywhere like masks, like masks with lace teeth, and on this day of hearts my father has a heart attack. Going for the newspaper in the morning sunlight by the Pacific Ocean. I flew down and drove his rental car to the mortuary. I was sick of goatees then and I'm sick of them now.

Your lungs with fluid; but your heart with something other. Levi and Gladys and all those in that blind canyon, all those in that last place of scalps and complicated slaughter, have reasons to seek escape, to feel betrayed, reasons to hop in a vintage Mustang or Meteor Rocket and hit the highway. To lose their lost skin beneath the mercury-lit overpass and lingering Northern Lights. To unfold wings and be thought considerate. Escaping escape. Pennsylvania. England. Terra Nova. The rest of us zooming under the prefab trestles are faking it, copping an attitude. Three blond heads chatter like cheerful wrens in the cracker-strewn backseat. (My father never allowed food in his cherished Oldsmobile, the Delta 88 I smashed.) I'm not saying anything to the boys. I am holding a wheel like it's a chisel, but I'm not escaping. I have my father's face, my father's hands, my father's heart. Ocean at my back, I'm going for a morning paper: The noises. A beautiful sweet breeze, sun-hot tiles and tiny reticulate leaves rushing toward me.

Love Bites and Little Spanks
Ramona Dearing

There's a trick to these storms—they come when Lenny is on the road. My husband is a dentist. He has the main office here, and a smaller one in Billy's Cove he goes to every Tuesday. There are two plastic chairs in the waiting area. The door next to one of them opens onto the room with the drill. The other room has a sofa-bed and TV, one of those big braided rugs covering some of the tiles. He stays over when the weather is down. Gracie does too. I can't prove it, because Lenny's only excuse for staying is that the roads are bad. But it's perfect—he won't lie to me. He doesn't have to. You don't take chances in the winter around here. Five people died the week before Christmas, a car and a tractor-trailer. Better to wait it out, that's why Lenny always takes an extra shirt with him.

I see them, the bar in the middle of the bed making them arch like dolphins, the TV on, the smell of burning teeth.

Yesterday I told him he could have her all the time. I meant it as a gift mostly. Also, I wanted him to remember me just long enough to tell me. I need his words, need him to say he is for her.

"What are you doing to me?" That's all he says before he swings for his lunch bag and goes out the door. He slips on ice at the bottom of the driveway, and almost falls. He rights himself, stands perfectly still, as if he's reading the graffiti on the hill across the harbour. He turns and nods to Sam next door and clomps away.

Gracie is my cousin. She has a beautiful ass, the kind

meant for love bites and little spanks. Her laugh stays with you the way the taste of licorice hangs on in your mouth. Gracie paints lupins and skeletons. She also does icebergs for the tourists. That's how she gets by, they pay whatever she asks. Greenish white, streaked with purple, big orange splotches for the puffins' feet. She used to sell fishing scenes, the houses and stages all tilting toward the waves. But it's the icebergs people want. She says if she did one right, instead of for money, it would be dark grey against black water. So grey you couldn't really see it, except you'd know it was there.

The top floor of her house and most of the second are closed off in the winter. The rest is always cold. She never gets her wood cut in time to dry properly and her electric heaters are a joke. She's hung moose antlers over her woodshed, they're covered in polka dots. She figures old Nish Collins down the road will hang her cat in revenge one day.

We were laughing drunk, putting on lipstick in the bathroom in the Star of the Sea hall when I told her. Kissing in his car, wriggling. That was a few years ago.

"You?" she said. "You?"

Lenny was in Quebec City at a dentists' convention. Every time I woke up, Herbert's hand was still on my hip. I decided I would tell Lenny as soon as he got back. But when I went to St. John's to get him at the airport he told me he'd been thinking we should get a dog, he'd do all the work.

Herbert phoned once after that, and I went over in the afternoon. We didn't say hello, just took our clothes off in the living-room. After, he said we could never be together again. He told me he had a cavity and didn't want Lenny's drill to slip. Then serious: "It's not me you're after. The two of you go walking, and everyone stops to watch you pass. The whole fucking town stares, but you never notice."

"What's this then?" I say. He shakes his head, sad. We kiss, one little breath after another.

When it blows, this place twitches and hums. Downstairs is not so bad, though the wind sucks at the stove damper like a tongue on a chalky peppermint. Upstairs, the bathroom fan clunks and the window in the front bedroom whines against the frame, even with rags pushed into the crack. There are strange easy moments between gusts, until another pushes at the house. The outside walls move then, just a little. The water in the toilet sloshes back and forth.

I usually pour a couple of rums to mute the din. Some nights I reach under the bed and pull out the fiddle Lenny's uncle Albert left him. I let it shriek until my elbow aches. Or I pluck out a lullaby the wind will never hear.

I've tried to learn as much as I could from Wilf Stokes. He comes for a visit sometimes, has one small nip before he'll play. His fingers mash the strings.

"It's like this," he says, but I can never see what he's doing. He listens with his eyes closed and doesn't say anything when I've finished. One time he said, "You'll be good enough one of these days."

I tutor his granddaughter, Jacinta, in exchange. Wilf says the more French she knows, the easier it will be for her to get work on the mainland. He says this as if Jacinta's leaving has already been arranged, although she still has another year of high school. She's hopeless, but sweet. Every time we meet, she tells me I have pretty hair. A couple of times her father has asked me to phone in an order for his hardware store to a company in Quebec. Plastic flowers for graves, Gore-tex jackets, skidoo parts.

I want to know when Gracie stopped thinking Lenny was boring. She used to roll her eyes when he talked, or lean back and let her head rest on the top of the chair.

He hangs the tea-towel over the oven door and sits at the table. I know he is comparing us. Our gumption, our tantrums. Me in a nightgown, her. The light in the kitchen is too bright. I hunch over the counter. The dough sticking to my hands makes my skin itch. If I could, I'd make snowflakes all day long, each one lacy, cut with very sharp sewing-scissors. The secret to a good one is to leave only tiny wisps of paper holding it together. It should be mostly air.

"Play for me," he says.

The smell of the bread is strong even in the living-room. I stand by the window, don't notice the frost has blocked the window until after I put the fiddle down. Lenny is in the kitchen. I hear the scrape of the oven rack, the soft thuds as he turns the bread out of the pans to cool. He stays in the kitchen until after I fall asleep.

Lenny's hands are too clean. He wears rubber gloves to do the dishes, and heavy cloth ones in the garden. He rubs his hands with lemon after chopping garlic. Lenny wants to be soothing, inoffensive as he pries open his patients' mouths and leans in. He says there is no way to erase the fear, even if the drill didn't make that noise. But his touch is warm. I know some of the wariness leaves as his fingers push down on their cheeks.

Coca-cola is stripping them down to the gums, he says, eating through their teeth like dry rot. At the strip mall last week he saw a baby with pop in its bottle. He went over and spoke to the mother.

"Right you are," the woman said, "but from what I understand, you've got some bad habits of your own to mind."

When he told me about it, he stared at the clock and said he was sorry. I heard later that it was Edith Butt he'd been talking to.

I floss every day. Sometimes I leave the bathroom door open so he'll hear the sound of the thread going pick-pick through my teeth. He doesn't care, he says my breath is good, but I've always thought you should bend a little, show someone you can move in their element with ease.

I phone Gracie. We go to the Pot-Luck, order eggrolls and hamburgers for lunch.

She says, "He's a lot better than I expected."

I know Gracie too well, I don't say anything.

"Do you want him back?" she says after Stella pours water in our glasses.

I stay quiet. Gracie picks up my hand. Her fingers jerk and jump. When I look back up to her face, she starts to giggle. I laugh too. A tiny piece of chewed burger lands on her cheek, but she ignores it. There's a steady buzzing, a low beep-beep outside. The lift bridge going up. I brush off her cheek. She leans forward across the table and talks softly.

"How about a three-way?" She wiggles her eyebrows.

"Before bingo or after?" I ask, and now we're bouncing our feet on the floor and Gracie says "Buy me a beer before I piss my pants."

Last night Lenny stayed away. I dreamt his Uncle Albert died all over again. A bunch of us stood around the casket, and every so often someone would say, "But he just got a job last week. He just got a job." And that made us all cry, waves and waves of tears.

Lenny phones in the afternoon.

"I won't be around much for a while."

"Oh," I say. And that's it.

Sometimes I wonder what the odds are of shuffling a deck of cards and having them come out in perfect order, the way they are in a brand new pack.

Marge's kitchen has a red kettle, red canisters, even red plastic measuring spoons hung on hooks. Cream yellow walls. She pushes a plate of date squares over to me.

I'm laughing, telling her at least if I ever need a root canal, it won't cost anything. Telling her I expect Gracie to plant my garden for me and feel so guilty she'll weed it for me too.

Marge says, "That's right honey, you just let it all out. You just keep going, honey, and work it out of you. You just let it come up."

The red and white boxes on her gingham tablecloth hurt my eyes.

"Just heave it out of you," she says.

When I walk home, the kids are shooting down the hill by the cemetery on their magic carpets. They try to run back to the top but their feet kick out and sometimes they slide all the way back down on their backs, the bright plastic scooting ahead of them.

Herbert gets up from the couch to get me another beer, and the floor shakes under his feet. He lives in a 35-foot trailer. The glass I'm drinking out of has a thumbprint on it. He sits at the other end of the couch, staring at the TV. It's on, but the volume's turned down.

"How can I do you?" he says. A car drives into a jungle sunset. We sit there. Then he says, "If it takes the sting away any, he didn't get a new woman. He's got the exact same woman. You and Gracie just traded places is all."

"Asshole."

"Exactly what she would have said." He's still grinning as I put my boots on. "But remember it's Liz I'm wild for."

We chose the house for its colour. A yellow that almost passes into orange. The house is the shape of a tea crate on its end. Out the windows of what used to be the parlour, you can see over the steel wall built to keep the waves from spilling against the houses when there's weather. The wall is rusting, the rust bleeds through the snow that's been pasted on by the wind. On a notepad I write, *I do not want to remember this time.* I rip out the page, fold it into a chunky wad and hide it at the back of my underwear drawer.

"I wasn't going to sleep with him," I tell Marge the next morning, "I wasn't going to sleep with him ever again. I just went there."

"You straighten up," Marge says. "You dipped your toes. Now you're complaining they're muddy."

"No," Gracie says. "You can't." Her nostrils flare wide. She's slouched forward with her breasts pushed up under her arms. "Does Lenny know?"

I want to get pregnant. I want my belly to jump away from my ribs, to flower crazily. If it's a boy, I'll get a sailor suit with baggy knickers made for him.

"I know I'm old," I tell Gracie.

"Are you asking for him back?"

"People will just keep saying what they've been saying,

76

only they'll have some more to say."

I want to cross my eyes and stick out my tongue. I want to go tobogganing. I am bursting, restless.

"Have you been careful?" she says.

"Have you?"

"I'm throwing up a little bit," she says.

It's getting dark out and her kitchen floor is cold. I make her some tea.

Lenny gives me a puppy for Christmas. "Cuter than I ever was," he says. The dog cries when there's a gale. He trembles against me and licks my hand.

Lenny takes down the moose antlers hanging above Gracie's shed. She's working on a painting, she's got it in a room on the second floor. She locks the door when she's done for the day. Her stomach is pointy.

We compare Sobeys stories. She's sure she hears people hissing at her, soft, under-the-breath hisses. I get the *you poor dear* looks.

I have four suitcases and a case of partridgeberry jam in the back of the car. The dog's chin bumps the edge of the window, paws scrabbling the seat. A job lined up in St. John's, at least for a few months. A translation contract for the government.

I'm leaving the house the way it is for now—blankets on the bed, the curtains up, placemats on the kitchen table. I give my plants to Gracie. She holds my hand and her tears wet down the fuzz on the baby's head. Ellen howls until she feels a nipple on her cheek.

"I'm the one who should be going," Gracie says.

The way she says it, it's not an apology. Lenny stands with his hands in his pockets. "At least show her your painting before she goes."

She shakes her head, and lowers it over the baby. When I pull out of the drive I feel Gracie's eyes on me, the way you feel an old woman watching you from behind a lace curtain.

"So you'll be leaving us for a while," Wilf Stokes says. Even though I told him a couple of weeks ago. He pats the top of the car. "Now don't come back from the city with an earring in your nose or any of that." I smile. He looks up, lets his head tilt and roll as if he's examining each cloud. "Looks like snow. You'll come right back if it gets messy, won't you." He hands me a bottle of moose.

"You stay steady," I say. The violin is in the back seat. I have a feeling I won't play again for a long time. When I get to the bridge, it's up. I put the car in park and wait. The dog barks after a couple of minutes.

Miss Pringle's Hour

Cynthia Flood

Fatherless girls are a particular concern. There are fourteen in the School. It is a great loss, a great absence, and not all of them have sensible mothers. Of course we mourn their soldier fathers who fell, but we must never think that these deaths and the terrible destruction of English cities were the sum of the War. *Cut is the branch that might have grown full straight*. Timorousness, a certain superficiality or frivolity, an unsuitable bravado, very often an excess of conscience: in fatherless girls, these are among the fruits of War. The teaching staff must be aware of this, in order to attempt corrective measures while the pliancy of youth still renders that possible. *Mem.* Spk Miss Michaelson re less crit Felicity's needlework.

July 8th, House Tennis Match, won by St. Hilda's. All the girls played very well, I thought. The tension of Speech Day has eased and our usual healthy attitude is with us again.

July 10th, Talk on Social Work as a Career, by Mrs. Edwards of the Jubilee Infirmary. Is it really twelve months since her last visit? Departing, Mrs. E commented that she likes visiting St. Mildred's because the girls' uniforms "have such a pretty old-fashioned look." ??? *Mem.* Ask RH.

Among the pedagogical theories of Mr. Neill at Summerhill, I recently came upon a tirade against uniforms. How little the man understands! Again and again, I have watched their beneficence at work. Angela: when she came to us in the Lower Fourth, miserably shy and anxious, our uniform sheltered her. She felt no longer vulnerable to notice, and thus reassured she was able to work. Term by term, she developed confidence in herself and in her School. I can see her now—or was it Anthea?—attaching her first monitor's pin to her tunic. Such care and pride. Her posture is much improved. She has reached the Sixth. She leaves her sleeves rolled up after Games, sets her School hat at a tilt. Within sight of her General Certificate, Amelia treats her beloved uniform casually because she believes herself ready to discard it.

Mrs. Edwards spoke well, although as usual I wish she would refrain from jokes. Senior girls about to leave School do not need such enticements in order to pay attention.

July 20th, Staff vs. 1st VI Tennis Match, won by 1st VI. I am not sure that Miss Barnes was pleased at this victory, in part at least the result of her excellent coaching of the girls. She is after all still young herself, but.

July 25th, End of Term. Everything went well, I thought, with only the customary few confusions of missed trains and forgotten articles of clothing. Of course the credit is entirely RH's. Her attention to detail is only matched by her skill in overall planning. Such efficiency is an important element in the School's *tone*, much changed since the days of my predecessor, that kindly woman of small authority. What would St. Mildred's do without Miss Ruth Hodgson, Assistant Head? HRH!

After tea, I began my inspection. The moss on the front steps has spread shockingly. I cannot think why Fitzgerald has not attended to this. Wear and tear are plain to see on the furniture in the junior and staff common rooms, but. As for the curtains—I chose that fabric in 1936. The piano-tuner must come. The forms, springboard and mats in the gym are shabby but serviceable. Miss Gregson has complained about the Science laboratory; I had thought she exaggerated yet am compelled to admit she is right. I should not like any member of Council to see the present condition of her equipment. The Lower Fifth's copies of *An Illustrated History of Modern Britain* are a disgrace. What has Miss Trout been thinking of? We cannot have this. Probably there will be no new edition for years. Not a decade since the War, and already this careless waste! The grounds look well. In this, Fitzgerald is meticulous. Reroofing St. Hilda's was very much the right decision. I did not reach the dormitories today.

Mem. Incl cmts re frugal in rmrks at Schl opening Sept. In rpt to Counc, emph rel betw eqpt/furn and qual educ, compare Clarendon. Spk Fitz re steps (muriatic acid?), Gwen S in Sept re abuse of piano, Trout re much closer superv of 5th. RH enq re new climbing ropes, arrange tuner, enq costs lab eqpt, meas for curtains & obtain fabric samples (chintz, *toile de Jouy?*).

Standing on the steps when all the girls have gone, looking out over the gravel drive and the Great Lawn, I find the silence fairly echoes. Miss Percival, who was with us for a term or two just after the War, once stood by me at this hour and said "Let the Irish vessel lie/Emptied of its poetry." Clearly she was wrong; Mr. Auden spoke of a dead fellow poet, not of a girls' school in England, nor do his lines quite rhyme, and many of our girls could not be termed at all poetic, yet I could find agreement with her. When full of girls, our Gym is not shabby.

Within a few days, the teaching staff, and Matron—whose sharp tongue I shall not miss—leave. There is then a great deal to do. RH and I inspect, make lists, attend to correspondence, take inventory, write accounts and reports. In Mrs. Howard's enormous kitchen, we cook scratch meals and carry them into RH's or my sitting-room. We prepare for my interview with Council. We ourselves interview prospective parents, girls, teachers. A new laundry must be selected. We must renegotiate with the baker.

We always enjoy our week in the Cotswolds. Each year, we hunt for our retirement cottage. RH lengthened her bird list considerably, with great pleasure. I had not been aware that there were so many different types of warbler.

Returning eagerly to School, we once again feel urgency. The telephone bell rings often. The post-bag swells. RH spends long hours with the timetable and I with the budget. Vans carrying staples, tinned goods, lavatory paper, chalk, soap, sheet music, notebooks, bedlinens, hockey sticks and foolscap drive up, displacing Fitzgerald's carefully-raked gravel (overlapping arcs, a style in Dublin, he says). The new teachers arrive.

September 20th, School reassembled. Mem. Spk Chair re bank overdraft, all teaching staff re new GC regulations, Fitz re not appear shirtless in term-time (a singlet at least), Matron re manner to new girls, Mrs. H re kitchen shelving.

September 25th. The Sixth and the Upper Fifth attended the Old Vic production of "A Winter's Tale" at the Royal. Meeting Dr. Chapple of Clarendon at the interval, I was pleased at the poise of our girls. Some of his boys were unnecessarily boisterous. Dr. C enquired re our university entrances. Of course Clarendon's size and endowments ensure a higher proportion than we can attain, but. The actors did very well, I thought.

September 30th, News-talk by Mr. Oliver Greene. The Canadian girl, Amanda Ellis, actually interrupted him to ask a question. No-one welcomes more warmly than I the post-war trend of arrivals from other Commonwealth (as we are now to call it) countries, but the difficulties cannot be denied. Apparently, the patterns of life followed by persons from the Caribbean living in our larger cities, unfortunately in their poorer quarters, are so different from those of native-born Britons as to cause considerable social disruption. Naturally there is nothing of this sort with Amanda, who is physically indistinguishable from her classmates, but.

Mr. Greene is prolix. Such a man will end his days in a residential hotel, one of the eccentric dodderers by the fire.

October 4th, Lantern Lecture on "The Romans in Britain," by Miss Laura Harvie, B.A., of the Historical Society. Funds simply must be found to purchase new equipment for such presentations.

Corresp: Old Girl Rosemary Hayton (Clarke) '37 wishes to endow a prize for best Senior essay on a nineteenth- or twentieth-century woman artist. Most generous, but I cannot think why she should wish thus to limit the subject-matter.

Mem. Ellis pts re elocution Amanda? RH enq lantern costs.

October 5th. Yesterday was tiring, yet after midnight I

was wakeful (uncomfortably warm). At my window, I looked out at the School—my reverie was broken by the unexpected sight of Mr G making his way across the Great Lawn and down the drive, crunching gravel with unnecessary vigour. The girls call him Mr. Grey. At such an hour, where can the man have been going? Only distasteful answers occur. Fitzgerald thus, yes, but Mr. Greene?

Mem. Spk Fitz, again, re suitable address—Miss Pringle, not simply Miss, which is appropriate in the unlikely circumstance of his speaking to one of the girls. These distinctions are significant. Unlike Mr. Neill, I insist upon outward and visible manifestations of respect. When a group of girls rises, as one, on my entrance, I am gratified, for in honouring my position they honour their own.

Oddly enough it was Mr. Greene who overheard the Chair of the Council's remark to Dr. Chapple. "Remarkable"—that was the term used—"remarkable, the improvement in tone at St. Mildred's since Pringle has been Head." RH was equally delighted. A good reputation among such men is invaluable to a small independent girls' School such as this. Of course Mr G told me so as to gain favour. He may think I do not know that. The man is a poodle.

The mention of *tone* is particularly satisfying. A School is far more than lessons. On Speech Day, we at St. Mildred's do not only award prizes for learning. We show the girls at various Games. We show them reciting, dancing, singing, acting, performing on instruments. We exhibit their needlework and paintings. The School Magazine, with its marvellous news of the Old Girls, is also given to parents...yet I almost pity those mothers and fathers. They know so little of their daughters!

Secret knowledge is not a small part of work such as mine. I know, for example, that Mr. Greene is Irish, a fearful man, and rightly fears for his post here. In her room, Miss Pruitt keeps a bottle of gin. Miss Lincoln is three years older than she owns to. Mrs. Howard's little manoeuvres with Purchasing were quite transparent. I made myself clear to her in turn. We had no more of that. A good cook is an asset to a School.

Other private knowledge is of a different character. Mrs. Wilmer's husband was killed in action; although some widows have done well with us, I now see she will never recover. In Maths, girls are at enough of a disadvantage without the weight of a distraught teacher. Pamela in Upper IV appears very able and must have first-rate coaching. Miss Flower has not grown up. There is a leaning to the sentimental. The Helen Hepworth matter was illustrative. However, her other traits—honesty, diligence, piety—are valuable, and not only in the girls' studies of Religious Knowledge. RH feels this strongly. RH herself: another secret. HRH! No-one else appreciates her.

Mr. Grey for Mr. Greene, Goody Two-Shoes for Miss Flower, Primp for Miss Pruitt, Lips for Miss Lincoln, The Oirishman for Fitzgerald: very apt the girls are. Miss L and Miss P's foolishness does no harm. (If I thought otherwise, they would not teach here.) Exposure to variety is valuable; we cannot all be serious scholars. Both teach conscientiously. They will not be long, I think, in finding husbands. For many, that is best. I confess to a resentment of L; she remarked, according to Matron, that "Miss H's frumpy clothes are copies of Miss P's, only paler." Yet the girls do very fine maps, I think.

October 22nd. Piano Recital by Miss M. Gates of the Conservatory. She played "The Merry Peasant." I remember Father humming that, and humming it myself during the dreary music at his funeral. November 1917. Thirty-six years ago! The deportment of some girls was poor. Helen H slouches ostentatiously.

After walking Fred and Nelly, RH complained of fatigue and retired early.

October 29th, Lecture on Australia by Mr. Alan Howell of Australia House, London. Many girls took a lively interest in this talk, accompanied by a short film, in colour. I do not like to think of them leaving England. Foolishly, I do not like them even to leave School, though as Seniors they must and do. Can there be a fuller world than here? Few see the richness. Lips chatted with Mr. Howell; the Lower Fourth are studying Australia.

Hodgson inevitably is Hedgehog. Pringle is Quangle. Hedgehog & Quangle. Like a pair of lawyers in Dickens, RH says! I do not in the least mind a sobriquet derived from Mr. Lear's charming nonsense, yet I see it as a rare failure of the girls' imaginations. Would I ever exclaim "That very few people come this way/ And that life on the whole seems far from gay!"? A Headmistress is by definition amongst people, and, while I would concur with Mr. Longfellow that "Life is real! Life is earnest!", I am not sad. For my subdued clothing I make no apology. Dr. Chapple may affect vivid ties and socks (mutton dressed as lamb, Father would have said), but it is not suitable for the Head of a small independent girls' school so to distinguish herself.

Mem. Spk Chair re overdraft, need for talks on career opportunities in Britain, lantern. Spk Mrs. H. re fish pie. RH arr GC examinations, enq costs new piano, rev proposals from house mistresses for new Prefects. Spk Helen H re self-respect, needs of School paramount, not malingering.

November 3rd, Half-term. I encouraged RH to rest. Much of my weekend went to a consideration of a rise in School fees.

November 10th, a group of 10 Old Girls visited the School for the weekend. Such visits are always gratifying.

November 20th, General Certificate started. Most will do well, although Miss Maywood is anxious about Gillian's Latin.

It is a great responsibility, preparing girls for the modern world. Much change is occurring in Britain, not all good, and confusing for the young. Lower moral standards and materialism are ubiquitous. At least we can now rest confidence in the Government, having made up for the embarrassment of the election immediately post-War. Such ingratitude! However, the stringencies of the War have only slowly lessened here. We cannot do all that should be done. We can only do our best. Even with rising costs of living, however, parents do continue to see our "extras" as desirable for their daughters, which pleases me. A boys' school, such as Clarendon, can raise fees without question, but.

November 29th, Performance of French Plays by Forms III, Lower IV, and Upper IV. As a girl, RH spent summers in France; she praised our girls' accents. I missed several bits of byplay, gestures and the like. Difficulties with vision are I suppose inevitable with age. One of the settees from the drawing-room was on stage; the plot required unsuitable bouncing about on this delicate piece of furniture, and Lesley was actually wearing her tennis shorts. Girls need to learn appropriate behaviour. I have always felt that St. Mildred's makes this lesson easy to learn, for the grace of the old buildings encourages good manners. Our integration of modernity must be respectful.

Complete fluency in French is unnecessary. We do not wish our girls to be mistaken for Frenchwomen.

Dr. Chapple once disparagingly remarked that it was a pity no scholarships were offered for Needlework. How little the man understands! Quite apart from its traditional feminine value, needlework requires concentration, physical skill, strict attention to detail and perseverance in the completion of a demanding task. The sight of Third Formers engaged on their first aprons and handkerchiefs therefore gratifies me. It is no exaggeration to say that the abilities involved built the Empire and may very well sustain the Commonwealth. Artistic talent may also be fostered.

Mem. Appt for eyes. Spk Secy of Council re fees on agenda, Matron re withdrawal of hot-water bottles not suitable discipline, Mme D. re settee, Amanda re VITamin not VITEamin. Spk Trout re order in classroom, again. RH begin revision of Clothing Lists, enq new Maths teacher, review menus with Mrs. H.

December 8th, St. Anne's House Party, a most pleasant occasion, although I may have a touch of 'flu, for the room seemed insufferably warm, although RH was quite comfortable.

December 11th, School Nativity Play.

December 14th, Prefects and Seniors attended the Clarendon College Dance. No untoward incidents occurred, although I shall not in future designate Miss T as chaperone.

December 15th, Council Meeting. Fees will rise, not by as

much as I would wish. To my surprise, the Chairman wishes to consider rises for the teaching staff. I cannot agree. Anyone who enters this profession—a calling, some might consider it—with a view to acquiring wealth is a fool. Careful management will enable those St. Mildred's staff who practise it to live in simple comfort. Room and board are, after all, provided. It was perhaps my annoyance that made me feel so distressingly warm.

RH and I agreed that we shall be glad to see the end of term. Her fatigue follows exertions that would formerly have seemed mild, or even pleasurable.

Mem. Appt eyes! Not done, in spite of earlier note.

December 16th, Carol Service. Miss Flower remarked that the girls' veils, rather than diminishing their individuality of appearance, accentuate it. Exactly. She went on, however, to compare nuns. I cannot approve (quite apart from the prerequisite beliefs). To withdraw so! To stand aside! No. Our girls must have opportunities to weave together *all* the strands of a full life—intellectual, vocational, social, domestic, even artistic.

December 18th, End of Term. Whether the girls avail themselves of such opportunities is to some extent beyond our control. Lead a horse to water, etc. However, the personal qualities of the staff—certainly as much as their teaching—exert a powerful influence. Mrs. Wilmer must go.

Snow fell. RH and I walked for a full hour before tea. Such an opportunity for uninterrupted conversation is rare. Afterwards, RH seemed quite puffed, and rested before dinner.

As usual in the holidays, there is much to do. A few days in London will be required. RH suggests a new School uniform! and proposes a visit to Neals'. We may manage a few days in the Cotswolds. At least, weather permitting, we shall take daily walks together.

January 1. The calendar New Year never seems as new as does the School year. Word of Father's death came on this day in '17, and of my brother's in '43. My poor Mother. RH pointed out blue tits, a chaffinch, blackbirds. The swans looked very white on the dark river edged with snow.

January 6th. The Royal's production of *Twelfth Night* opened on this date, appropriately. RH enjoyed herself very much. All the actors did well, I thought.

Neals' has sent sample designs for new uniforms. I wrote to Mrs. Wilmer. RH complained of pain in arm and rested after tea.

January 12th, near Burford. We may, at last, have found a suitable cottage. I hardly dare to write this.

January 17th. School reassembled.

January 20th, Talk on Careers by Miss Macnaughton of the Ministry of Labour. Matron described her as "hardbitten," not a term I would myself employ, but her personality was less than engaging. A great pity. Some girls—Victoria, Janice, Eleanor, Anne—simply ceased to listen, yet I know that Janice has a genuine interest in veterinary medicine.

I thought of her today when in town. Eileen as usual set my hair very nicely, and as usual I thought how dreadful her Irish accent is and how glad I am that no St. Mildred's girl—barring utter disaster—will ever need to earn her living thus.

Dr. Ingram recommends spectacles. I returned to School feeling depressed. RH as always was most solicitous. HRH.

January 31st, Lantern Lecture on "The Geology of Britain," by Mr. D. S. McKee, of Cambridge. Our new equipment makes a great difference in such a presentation, especially on a topic not of automatic interest to girls. The young man did open vistas about future work. Valerie was enthusiastic. Of course Lips and Primp were at the dais moments after he concluded. I should not be surprised to see Valerie return to us one day, teaching a Science. I have often predicted which Old Girls will return, which will send their daughters here. Not all by any means were prefects or prize-winners.

Mem. Birthday present for HRH.

February 10th, Lecture by Miss Penelope Seaman on the Maryhill Missions in Kenya, Rhodesia and Nigeria. The name smacks of Catholicism, yet those involved—only some are RC—do fine work. We are of course a long way from "They call us to deliver/Their land from error's chain," but Africa *is* in a bad way. We must help. This is important for the girls to see. Some were alarmed at Miss Seaman's comments on the Mau Mau. The ingratitude, after all the British have done in Kenya, seems absolutely shocking.

I regret having written thus of Catholicism, which is simply at the furthest point on the Christian spectrum.

RH is delighted with her camera.

Mem. Spk Chair re uniforms, teaching staff re Spring morale slump, Vicar re Confirmation class, Trout re classroom atmosphere, Helen H re poor posture, Wilmer re replacement. RH arr GC exams, enq costs new gym eqpt, draft fees letter to pts.

Really, a new science *Building* would be most desirable.

February 15th, News-talk by Mr. Oliver Greene. Can the man become any more desiccated in manner or appearance? He is undeniably well-informed, however.

RH and I speak rarely of Burford, except as required owing to correspondence from agent, bank, etc.

The new uniforms engage me greatly. I am sure that RH is right in thinking it is time, not of course for the sake of change itself, but to make the girls' dress better suited to who they are: young women of the second half of the twentieth century. Daily, we consider Neals' sketches over coffee or before retiring. The School colours will not alter, of course.

How best to introduce the new clothing? Should an incoming Third Form be the first outfitted, and so lead the way up the School? However, not all girls enter in the Third. A parti-coloured effect would be poor, in the School Photograph for example, or at Away matches. Morale would suffer. I would not wish to put parents to the expense of *two* uniforms during a daughter's years at St. Mildred's, but.

RH thinks I am going through the change. I have been most reluctant to write this.

February 21st, House Dancing Competition, won by St. Anne's. All the girls danced very well, I thought.

Owing to colds and a nasty gastro-intestinal infection, the San is full. Matron is better in such a demanding situation than when there is little illness. On the whole, not a good trait.

A talk (our third) with Mrs. Wilmer today. I wish altering my decision were possible, but. I shall of course provide a good reference. In individual tutoring, she would do very well.

If the new uniforms were immediately introduced in the Third Form, the entire School would be newly clothed by my retirement at 60. Why on earth should Dr. Chapple be able to continue as Head for five more years than I?

We have concluded the purchase of the cottage at Burford. In the change, my poor Mother became red and most distressed. There is simply no reason why I should not continue. I have never seen more clearly what St. Mildred's needs nor how to provide it. Some plans simply cannot come quickly to fruition. HRH. Without her calm I should be even angrier. The cottage garden offers great potential for her. Occasional visits should be possible in term-time. We shall be there, and here. We shall.

March 1st, Form Gymnastic Competition, won by Upper VI.
All the girls did very well, I thought.

If I must retire at 60, I shall not see Valerie's return.

Mem. Hair appt. My hair does not hold a set as formerly. A neat appearance is essential. Eileen suggests that I reduce the interval between appts from six weeks to four.

March 2nd, Half-term. To Burford. We attended service at what will be our church. Afterwards, RH asked me why, since I do not believe, I sing the hymns with such enthusiasm.

On the village war memorial, RH noted two examples of a father dying in the First and a son in the Second World War, as in my family.

Buds are visible on the trees and shrubs. The Windrush is very pretty. RH took many photographs.

March 20th, Good Friday. The Senior Prefects read the Lessons very well, I thought.

Miss Barnes and Miss Pruitt desire a rise in pay. They believe themselves entitled to the same salary as the junior masters at Clarendon. RH is as always tolerant. I am compelled to admit she is right that young women do well to be concerned about their financial future, but. Alone, neither RH nor I could afford the cottage. I positively dread the little residential hotels one sees all over England. A terrible terminus. HRH. But really, small independent girls' schools simply cannot pay such salaries. Always, the good of the School must be paramount.

Becoming accustomed to spectacles takes time.

Mem. Once more, see Miss T re order in classroom.

March 25th, Council Meeting. Uniforms, salary increases, New English Bible, new Science Building, Speech Day, application from Nigerian businessman in Manchester for his daughter, drains. We all regret that the new General Certificate only records a pass, however good the individual marks may be. This levelling down, rather than an encouragement to aim high, is most unfortunate.

RH indisposed. Pain in upper arm again.

March 28th, Lecture on the Mystery Plays, by Miss Ellen Hurrell, B.A.. Dr. Chapple attended, with a friend, as did the Vicar and Curate. Mr. Greene has just arrived at the School. A little reception afterwards was thus quite lively. Unaccountably, I introduced Miss Pruitt as Miss Percival, which annoyed me.

Dr. C says he regards Speech Day at Clarendon as "the crown of the year." I cannot agree. Certainly then the School *displays* itself most fully, but *is* not most itself.

There are days during the cycle of the year when I feel the School running at full tide—the first At Home match in the autumn, the Carol Service, the spring sitting of the General Certificate, the annual School Photograph. Sometimes I must make an announcement in Dining Hall, as when the King died. Then the School is one. This is my hour. Or I may pass through the central hall at half-past ten of a weekday. Latin verbs murmur in the Lower Fourth. Light flashes from needles in the sewing-room. Mme. Dutheil is giving a *dictée*. In beginning chemistry, beakers tap and chink. Outside, Fitzgerald mows the Great Lawn. Someone is practising scales on the piano, and tripping over B. No-one sees me. All my girls and mistresses are here, at

School. That is my hour, my year's crown. Or an individual girl may do something which says *St. Mildred's*. A new prefect tells me of an untoward activity in her dormitory. A Third Form girl wins a battle over nail-biting, and shows me her clean hands. A sixth-former writes an essay so good that a scholarship which could transform her life moves within reach. Parents never live such hours.

If I must retire at 60, I am not likely to see the completion of the Science Building.

Dr. C, in commenting on the *Plays*, used the term *quaint*, pejoratively. I do not approve of such light-hearted dismissal of Christianity's many profound expressions. Just as I wish our girls to refrain from shorts in our drawing-room, I wish them to inhabit the house of their country's history—which includes Christianity—respectfully. Indeed, I later told RH, I do sing some hymns, or parts of some hymns, with enthusiasm—for example, "When Duty calls, or Danger,/ Be never wanting there." The dangers incurred in running a School are great, given the responsibilities we bear for the future of the country, although duty is more prominent to the lay eye. "Jerusalem" and "St. Patrick's Breastplate" are also stirring.

April 2nd, First Meeting of Confirmation Class. Eleven girls will participate.

Passing the Lower Fifth, I overheard the few last words of Miss Pruitt's exposition of Iambic Pentameter, followed by a recital: "Look *on* my *works*, ye *Mighty, and* despair!"

Mem. Write acceptance for Nigerian girl.

April 3rd, End of Term. Two hundred girls plus mistresses and staff departed successfully. RH now has Fitz carry the trunks up to the dormitories three days in advance, instead of two. This seems to make a great difference.

After five terms, I have concluded that Miss Trout cannot—at her present stage of development—be a better disciplinarian. *If* she has the capacity to progress, she must do so elsewhere. I regret this; she is an Old Girl and takes a very lively interest in her subject. However, a teacher must command respect, and Miss T is too inclined to a girlish impulsiveness.

In RH's view, almost ten years post-War we must consider repainting the dormitories. She says it is not good for the girls to rest in such worn, shabby quarters. Kindness itself. HRH.

Miss Barnes wishes the girls themselves to elect the captains of the netball, tennis and swimming teams. No-one appreciates more than I the advantages and burdens of democracy, nor of the need for youth to gain experience in both, but. RH is in favour. We discuss this and much else at Burford.

Holiday too short. Much enjoyed our country walks, though sometimes had to rouse RH to accompany me. I was glad for Nelly and Fred's insistence. Greater spotted woodpecker, snipe, pipit. RH enjoyed her camera. Several pleasing studies of our new home resulted. During our summer holidays, I think a visit to the doctor would be in order for RH. Certainly there can be none of this change nonsense for her, she is younger than I, but she lacks energy. Father used to jolly me along, when I moped. If RH feels tired, I encourage her to walk further. Better to hearten. NB binoculars for her next birthday.

Returned to School to find Neals' firm estimate: far too high. Their prices have unaccountably risen since Christmas. We really cannot have this. I hope to present the designs for the new uniform on Speech Day.

Inspected grounds. Wall at entrance and fencing by daygirls' bicycle shed need minor repair. A tramp may have been sleeping in garden shed. Fitz disclaims any knowledge. Made it clear to him that we simply cannot have School made use of by men incapable of managing their lives to the extent that they have no home. Lawn and flowerbeds are immaculate. F wishes to enlarge two borders.

I mislay my spectacles frequently. RH suggests a cord.

Interview with Miss T, who took it well.

In—I trust—final talk with Mrs. W., I made it abundantly clear that since she has never signed any contract with the School, her hopes for legal redress must be slim.

Mem. Spk Fitz re kitchen garden enlargement, kale, rasp

canes, reduce sprouts. Dormant oil to damsons. Agree borders. Spk Mrs. H re summer fruit *not* always stewed. RH
advert: Maths, Hist.

May 1st, School re-assembled.

*May 7th, Piano recital by Mr. Andrew Mornay of the Con-
servatory.* Handsome is as handsome does.

*May 9th, Talk by the Reverend Geoffrey Hart on the Church
Pastoral-Aid Society.* To the best of my recollection, he gave
last year's talk verbatim.

At Staff Meeting today, acceptance of Nigerian girl subject of lengthy discussion. I spoke of the Commonwealth
and of our opportunity, indeed our duty, to share the very
best of England.

Mem. Spk Chair re Speech Day plans, Old Girls Assn re
funds new Science Building, Miss F re Confirmation class,
Mrs. H re quality of bread poor. Spk Head Girl re poor beh
of two senior prefects during Talk. RH tel secy of CP-AS
and speak frankly (after sending letter of thanks).

May 15th, School Photograph Taken. The event went very
well, I thought. Today's slight cloudiness should lessen the
number of girls in the photograph squinting against the
sun.

*May 19th, Lantern Lecture on the Brontes of Yorkshire, by
Mr. Leslie Morton of Oxford.* New equipment again is entirely successful. Branwell Bronte appears to have been a
wastrel. Mr. Morton was, I think, rather older than Miss L
and Miss P had anticipated.

The Spring is delightful, though I find that I spend term-
time almost entirely indoors. RH of course walks dogs daily.

May 20th, Old Girls' 'At-Home'. A very satisfactory occasion, although RH retired long before the reception was
over. Her arrangements made the whole event smooth.
HRH.

Mem. Spk Fitz re not appearing shirtless in term-time—a
singlet at the very least.

*May 26th, Talk by Mrs. Rawlinson of the Royal Jubilee on
"Nursing as a Career."* A most capable administrator, she
makes an excellent impression. Nursing is not the profession which I most gladly see our girls enter, but. To my

annoyance, her name slipped from my memory as I introduced her. I cannot have this.

June 1st, Half-term. Hair appt. Eileen looks forward to a visit home to Galway. Her manner is most pleasant. A great pity.

Interviewed three prospective teachers of Mathematics, one of whom turned out to be a man! Cannot understand how this happened. RH also at a loss. An inoffensive young person, but. I have no objections to men as visitors to the School; they can bring in another perspective.

Interviewed two candidates for History, and shall have no difficulty making this decision. Miss Birkenstall might as well be an Old Girl.

Corresp: Letter from father of Nigerian girl. Her arrival in September will take very careful handling indeed. RH and I will discuss at length, at Burford.

June 10th, All music students attended performance by London Philharmonic Orchestra, on tour. RH enjoyed this very much.

June 16th, General Certificate started. Most of the girls will do well, I think.

June 20th, Expedition by motor coach to Abbey ruins. Miss Trout was in charge. I think many girls truly learned. However, for disciplinary reasons, I had to see no fewer than five girls in my office after the excursion. We really cannot have this.

The School Photograph includes only one squinter, Helen H. I am quite sure that this was deliberate. RH looks very well.

June 25th, Confirmation. Ten girls were confirmed. Miss Flower and the Vicar felt that Jennifer's confusion over consubstantiation made her an unsuitable candidate. Next year? Her mother is RC, which may account for the difficulty. According to RH, Miss F handled this rather awkward situation well. The Bishop Walmesley took tea on the Great Lawn with the candidates and their parents. RH and he spoke of her father, in old age a petty canon at the Cathedral where the Bishop began his career. RH was touched at his recollections of her father singing, off-key.

Hard work from now until the end of term will enable us

to spend almost a fortnight at Burford.

Only the major enterprise of Speech Day remains. Netball, tennis and swimming are well in hand, and the elected captains of the senior teams are those I would myself have chosen. The uniform project is underway. Very few parents are in arrears, I understand from RH, and the Chairman tells me that the new member of Council takes an especial interest in Sciences for girls since his own daughter is a chemist. He is enthused at the prospect of a Building. Several times weekly, Mrs. Howard presents attractive dishes of fresh fruit. Pamela's mathematical abilities appear exceptional. Miss Maywood reports that three girls in the Fifth show real promise not only in Latin but also in Greek. The Upper Fourth is, according to Miss Michaelson, the most competent group of needlewomen she has seen since 1938. All in all, it will be a pleasure to make my Report on Speech Day on the 10th.

June 29th, House Tennis Match, won by St. Anne's. All the girls played very well, I thought.

The cord for my specs is most helpful. HRH!

Mem. RH enq re new tennis Cup; there is very little space left for the engraving of winners' names.

July 4th. Ruth Catherine Hodgson died in her sleep. Her heart failed. I found her in her bed at 6:16 this morning.

July 8th, Miss Hodgson's funeral. The Choir sang beautifully, I thought. The Bishop was most kind. Everyone was most kind. Of course I had not expected to see him again so soon. He spoke of God's will. I cannot agree.

July 10th, Speech Day. Although the Chairman spoke most appreciatively of all that RH did for St. Mildred's, the Day remained, as she would have wished, a celebration of the School. More parents than ever attended. Dr. Chapple was complimentary.

July 11th. One week.

July 18th. Two weeks. Each day, Matron takes Nelly and Fred for a long walk. I have misjudged her.

July 25th, End of Term. Three weeks. I shall not leave the School, but rather attend to the Burford sale from here.

Miss Lincoln offered assistance in inspecting classrooms,

gym, etc. She would be prepared to rearrange her holiday plans. I declined, with thanks. I have misjudged her also. Misjudged. HRH. HRH. Fitz has found a good home, on a farm, for Fred and Nelly.

September 15th. Eleven weeks. Miss Hunnicutt and Miss Birkenstall, new Maths and History respectively, arrive today. Cutt and Stall. Hedgehog & Quangle. Like Dickens lawyers. The new secretary's arrangements for meeting trains are thoroughly unsatisfactory. The Nigerian girl waited an hour, alone.

Mem. Arrange Sixth outing *As You Like It*. Spk Chair re agenda for Sept mtg, all teaching staff re School spirit, Miss Hunnicutt re Pamela schlshp, Fitz re kitchen garden wall (repoint), Prefects re set example punctuality. RH no, new secy review fee payments, prep Hall seating plans, arrange removal RH furn & paint office. RH. HRH. HRH.

Remembering Manuel

David Henderson

"Have you been married before, Linda?" Mother asks. "I'm afraid Edward hasn't told me much about you." My mother is more bent and wrinkled than the last time I saw her, but no less sharp for all her 80-odd years. She's seated at the head of table, opposite me. There are four of us for dinner, Linda to Mother's right, Consuela to her left. Linda and I were married two days ago in Toronto, and have stopped over in Vancouver en route to Hawaii so Mother can meet her latest daughter-in-law.

"It's my third time," Linda says. "Same as Edward. Third time lucky."

"I do hope so. Are there children from your previous marriages?"

"None living at home."

"And you're a career woman. A TV journalist."

"That's right." Linda plays with her white-wine glass, long nails clicking on the crystal.

"I hope you don't mind me asking all these questions," Mother says.

"No, of course not."

"It's just that I'd like to know you a bit better."

"And I, you," Linda says. "Edward isn't all that forthcoming about his family."

"Isn't he, now."

Consuela clears away the remains of the shrimp and papaya hors d'oeuvre. Linda watches her. She's not sure how to place Mother's long-time companion, a robust woman in her mid-sixties.

After serving the cold sherry consommé, Consuela resumes her seat.

"I've been admiring your paintings," Linda says to Mother. She indicates the pictures on the dining-room walls. "Are they your work?"

My mother looks around as if noticing them for the first time. "Yes, they are," she says. My favourite, done when I was a small child, is a near-Fauvist rendering of a profusion of wild orchids. The other half-dozen are tropical scenes and landscapes. So different from the tidy still-lifes and formal gardens of recent years.

"They're lovely!" Linda says. "The colours! Edward didn't tell me you were such an accomplished artist."

"Why, thank you," Mother says. Her work, in fact, hangs in several collections. "They were done when we lived in El Salvador."

"Edward said you spent much of your life there."

"From 1936 until my husband's death."

Linda adopts the puzzled look she's perfected for her TV interviews. "What brought you there in the first place? It would seem an unusual choice."

Mother corrects the alignment of her cutlery. "There were business opportunities my husband wished to take advantage of."

What my mother doesn't mention is that her family practically drove her, a rebellious young artist, from England—disowned her publicly when she married Karl Schreiber, a well-to-do German of questionable reputation. With Europe moving toward war, the newlyweds left for El Salvador, where my father's sister and brother-in-law, Katerina and Hans Kroeger, were already established. After the war, my mother's family attempted to smooth matters over, but were rebuffed. Forgiveness doesn't come easily to Mother. She's never returned to England. When Father died seventeen years ago, it was to Vancouver she came.

Linda's still looking at the paintings. "I'm just thinking how different your landscapes and flowers are from what's been in the news." Her tone is confidential, inquiring. "All that fighting and killing."

"So awful," Mother says. "It makes me sick at heart. It was such a lovely land with its mountains and coffee plantations, and gardens no palette could match!"

"You must have wonderful memories. I'm surprised Edward talks so little about his time there."

"It was long ago," I say. "I was only seven when I was sent off to boarding-school. I didn't return all that often." It's also a part of my life I've tried not to think about.

Linda ignores me. "Where did you live in El Salvador? The capital?"

"Close by. Soon after arriving, we found a wonderful place on three acres of land, near San Benito on the outskirts of San Salvador. The garden was a marvel! It came complete with a gardener who lived in a cottage at the back of the property." Mother turns to me. "You remember Manuel, don't you, Edward?" When I fail to respond, she says to Linda, "He was the best gardener I ever had. The garden was his life. He had a wonderful touch, could make anything grow. After Manuel, I could never find anyone as good, and the garden suffered. It still gives me a pang when I think of it." Her eyes seek mine. "Surely you remember Manuel."

Consuela darts me a warning look. This, as she knows well, is dangerous territory. I can tell she's displeased with Mother for resurrecting Manuel. I concentrate on the consommé.

"You used to follow him about the garden for hours on end." A note of insistence has entered Mother's voice. "Drove your nanny silly."

I can no longer hold back the memories that rush in, some long buried. The great house where we lived, servants whispering in the shadows by the interior arches, and the tile floors across which, at night, hairy tarantulas sometimes scuttled. Then, the garden—my favourite place. I knew every corner of it, went there as often as I could. And Manuel—sturdy, patient Manuel—was a part of it as he pushed the handmower against the resistant grass, weeded

beds of begonias, roses and violets, trimmed the shrub-
bery—frangipani and gentians—and pruned the trees—
guava, maquilishuat, medlar, lemon. Such richness of
growth to be contained.

I was forever following along behind him, full of questions. Once, I remember, I asked him why he was cutting
the fading flowers off a spiraea. I was standing beside him
as he knelt to the task. An earthy odour emanated from
him, laced with tobacco and sweat. He turned his broad,
kind mestizo face toward me, a face that turned expression-
less only when others approached. "Because," he said, "the
old must give way so the young have space to live, niño."
Niño is what he called me. Not Eduardo like my nanny,
Eduard like my father, or Edward like Mother. Niño. "Does
that mean that you're going to die?" I asked, and he
laughed. "I'm not that old," he said. And another time, I
asked him why a hydrangea went from pink to blue when
he transplanted it. "It's unhappy at being uprooted," he
said, "just like anybody." And when I asked too many
questions, he'd simply say, "Because that's the way it is,
niño." I thought him very wise.

Mother's wrong, though, about my nanny (another curious resurrection). Alicia seldom minded when I skipped off
to the garden to find Manuel.

My mother's eyes are still on me. I can feel them. "You
must remember him, Edward," she says. "He was very patient with you." Clearly, she's not going to let me off the
hook, as if she needs some sign of complicity from me.

"Edward?" Linda says. She's puzzled by my silence.

I look up at my mother. I can no longer find in her any
trace of that restless young Englishwoman who gave birth
to me in Central America, but then I don't know her particularly well. Even her move to Vancouver in the mid-
nineteen-seventies hasn't changed that. She dislikes travel,
and my business in Toronto doesn't leave me much time to
come out here.

"Yes," I say, finally, "I remember him. He always wore a
straw hat. Sometimes, he'd take you and Consuela on a tour

of the garden to show you what he was doing. He'd gather bouquets for the house, but he always had a special flower for Consuela."

"That's sweet," Linda says.

Consuela gives me a double-barrelled blast with her dark eyes, then looks down. "He was a kind man," she says. "He deserved better."

"Just so," Mother says, and then to Linda, "Now, there's a tale...."

"Do you remember your parrot, Mother?" I ask. "The green one Father gave you? He had a yellow head, and red and yellow markings. He'd sit on your arm and you'd talk to him. You called him Pablo, after Picasso."

But Mother is not to be diverted. "Would you like to hear Manuel's story?" she asks Linda.

"I'd love to." Of course she would. It's for something like this she's been poking about.

"Aunt Mary, I don't think this is an appropriate topic for the dinner table," Consuela says. Her voice is firm.

Mother waves a hand. "Nonsense, dear. I have no intention of being distasteful."

Consuela gets abruptly to her feet, her chair nearly tipping, and clears the table in preparation for the main course. Plates clatter.

Mother gazes at Consuela a moment before she says, "You must think I'm being difficult."

"That's not...."

"I have no wish to upset you, dear, but you must let me go on a bit about the past. At my age, it's of more interest than the future. Try to understand."

"Would you like some claret?" Consuela asks Linda. "We're having roast beef."

Consuela was an attractive, mature fifteen when she became a lady's maid to Mother. Her family was mestizo, from the countryside, and this was her chance to escape the poverty that otherwise awaited her. Mother, for her part, continually encouraged Consuela to better herself, provided her with tutoring, assisted her in many ways.

Now, Consuela is Mother's companion. She still looks after Mother, but as a friend. In fact, she's been Mother's closest confidant for a number of years, and her influence in this relationship has grown steadily. When Mother dies, I suspect Consuela will get half the estate. I don't begrudge her a penny. She's devoted her life to my mother, and, besides, there's enough to go round.

Mother begins her story, builds it gradually. She mentions something of Manuel's rural origins and how he came to the city, and then dwells on the changes and additions to the garden she had him make. She recalls, for instance, the veranera she had him plant against the sunniest walls of the house, and how it climbed bearing clusters of small flowers—splashes of orange, pink and white.

As Mother talks, Consuela brings in bowls of mashed potatoes, broccoli with hollandaise, and carrots, and, last, a platter of sliced roast beef and Yorkshire pudding. She's under control again, and serves everyone with the confidence of a hostess, interrupting Mother's story whenever necessary. Nothing of the long-ago servant remains.

As lady's maid, Consuela attended my mother's every need, helped her dress and undress, bathed her, saw that her clothes were clean. When Mother set up her easel in the garden, Consuela was there at her shoulder, ready to be of assistance, watching in wonder as colours exploded on the canvas. And when my mother went farther afield to paint, Consuela accompanied her, lugging her equipment as they dashed off to a waiting car.

Every morning, weather permitting, Consuela carried Pablo, Mother's parrot, out onto the terrace and placed him under the awning. An Amazon parrot, he called us by name, mimicked fragments of conversation, even made his own comments. He'd say, "Mary gone painting," or "Where's Alicia?" or "Don Carlos busy!" Mother and Consuela could handle him, and I could scratch his head, but he'd bite anyone else who came too close. Father included.

My time until lunch was taken with lessons—English,

German, arithmetic—taught by a succession of pale, nervous male tutors. Lunch, a languorous affair, was served on the terrace. How well I remember those lunches, seasoned by scents from the garden! Father was often there. He was a tall man with a pencil moustache and dark, slicked-back hair. Handsome as a matinée idol.

Alicia, my nanny, and Consuela were permitted to join us for that meal. Alicia's family were refugees from the Spanish Civil War. She had large eyes, fair skin and long undulating black hair. She and Consuela didn't get along.

Helen Sayed sometimes joined us as well. A friend of Mother's and an amateur painter, she was English, married to a Lebanese businessman whose interests, reputedly, were shady. I recall one particular lunch when Helen, who had no children of her own, took me on her knee and asked me if I knew the story of *Alice-in-Wonderland*. She was tanned from the painting expeditions she and Mother made to the countryside, and smelled of lavender. I said I knew some of it, with the rabbit hole and the Cheshire cat. "Ah," she said, "but that's not the best version!" And she proceeded to entertain me with her own Central American rendering, in which the rabbit hole became a trapdoor spider's hole, and the Cheshire cat a jaguar, with terrifying consequences for Alice. My mother was amused, but not Father. Later that afternoon, while hiding from Alicia in the garden, I saw Helen and Mother walking together, out of sight of the house. They were holding hands the way younger women in that part of the world sometimes did.

In the evenings, my parents often entertained—the rich coffee-growing families, businessmen, artists, doctors, top government officials, and a scattering of the military. Mother loved giving these dinners or parties—thrived on the excitement and gaiety. She created a stir in a country where women were expected to be more demure. As for my father, these gatherings were where he transacted much of his business.

I was forever sneaking out of my room after bedtime to spy on these goings-on, or if there were no guests, to prowl about, pretending I was a black jaguar. On these sorties, I saw things I wasn't supposed to. Consuela and Manuel standing in the shadows just off the terrace, not talking, not touching, but standing so close I could not have passed my hand between them.

Consuela brings the gravy around, serves the wine. We all compliment her on the food. She is an excellent cook. She smiles politely at Linda's plaudits, doesn't respond to Mother's.

In the hot season, we sometimes went to stay with Uncle Hans and Aunt Katerina by Lake Ilopango, which was only a few kilometres from San Salvador. The lake is large, volcanic in origin. Mother painted a lot during these visits.

We went there for a few days in 1943, the year of the climax of Mother's story. I was six at the time. I hated the visit. Things were starting to go badly for Germany in the war, and my older cousins bullied me, called me "Engländer." Uncle Hans was particularly upset by the reverses in Russia, ranting on about them and pushing my father off the neutral stance he generally took on the war. This effectively isolated my mother, who stormed out of the chalet saying that if they were so concerned for their homeland and their bloody Austrian postcard painter, then they ought to go back and take up arms. Later, everyone calmed down, but the damage had been done. We went back to the city, and, from then on, the two families rarely got together. Father, though, continued to see his sister regularly.

Mother is finally coming to the crux of her story. "One day," she says, "Manuel didn't appear. We thought nothing of it at the time. Occasionally, he would disappear for a day or so and say afterwards there had been an illness or death in his family. But this time, four days passed, and still no sign of him!"

And then there were the bees. How could I have forgotten

the bees? They used to bother Mother when she painted in the garden, attracted by her perfume, the paints or her clothes. Consuela had to shoo them away. The bees, though, fascinated me, and I would scoop one from a flower, gently closing my fist around it. The bee would remain quiet, its bristles tickling me. Then I would open my hand and study its eyes and colours and wings until it flew away. I was still doing this at the time of Mother's story, although I never did it in front of my parents, Alicia or the servants. Consuela saw me once, by accident. She looked surprised, but said nothing.

Manuel, though, often saw me picking up bees. When I asked him, "Manuel, can you do this?" he replied, "When I was your age, niño, I went to the bees' nests to eat the honey, and they would cover my arm. But no longer. Only those with the heart of a child can take up bees." As he spoke, I thought I could see, for an instant, through to the core of things, and I knew he was very wise.

"Finally, Edward's father sent a servant to check Manuel's cottage," Mother says. "Well, you just can't imagine the bedlam! There were screams from the garden and all the servants rushed to see what the matter was. Such confusion! At last, one of them returned to say they'd found Manuel in his cottage—dead! He'd been murdered and stuffed in a rain barrel!"

"Murdered!" Linda exclaims. She wasn't expecting the story to take quite this turn. "How? What happened?"

"Apparently he'd been playing cards and drinking chicha with some men. An argument erupted and he was killed. His throat slit. The men stuffed him in a barrel and fled. It was perfectly dreadful!"

I am listening carefully to Mother's story now. Significant differences between her recollections and mine are beginning to surface.

To start with, I was the one who discovered Manuel's body.

Those times when Manuel disappeared for a day or two,

the garden seemed incomplete. But he always returned, and it was as if he'd never been away. This time, however, when he still hadn't appeared by the fourth day, I became worried and decided to look for him at his cottage. What if he were sick? My parents had always sternly forbidden me to go there, but they weren't around to stop me. Mother was off on a painting expedition with Helen and Consuela, and Father was not to be disturbed. As for my nanny, she was off having one of her periodic naps.

I slipped away from an English lesson, telling the tutor I had to go to the bathroom. As I stole across the terrace, Pablo squawked, "Eduardo, English! Come to my room!"

"Shhh!" I hissed, and raced through the garden to Manuel's cottage, apprehension overtaking me. When I opened the unlocked door, the putrid odour of decay hit me. Putting my hand over my nose, I entered the kitchen, saw the trail of dried blood leading to a large barrel. Mesmerized, I dragged a chair over, climbed up and lifted the lid. It was Manuel, his head twisted so that the side of his bloated face and the gaping wound to his throat were visible. The sight and the stench immediately overcame me, and I stumbled outside and vomited as if my stomach were bottomless. When the heaving finally stopped, I ran straight to the house, tripping and tearing through the flowerbeds in my way.

One of the kitchen servants came out on the terrace as I approached (had I called out?) and asked what was wrong. As I rushed by, panting and sobbing, I wailed that Manuel was dead.

The servant gave a cry, hands to her face, and Pablo screeched, "Manuel's dead! No flower for Consuela!"

I rushed up to my nanny's room on the top floor in the far corner of the house. Franco, father's manservant, tried to block me as I dashed past him on the stairs, but he was encumbered by a tray. He called angrily for me to stop, set the tray down and came after me. Too late! I reached the door and burst into my nanny's room.

"Alicia...!" I cried, and then froze. I could hear Franco's footsteps approaching. They stopped outside the doorway.

Light poured into Alicia's room through open windows, and the semi-sheer curtains billowed in the breeze. Her white rattan bed was at one end of the room, and a matching dressing-table and chest of drawers at the other. By the windows, partially obscured by the floating curtains, was an upholstered chair without arms. On it sat my father, wearing his black silk bathrobe. Astride his lap, facing him, head thrown back, was Alicia. She wore a loose white satin dressing-gown, and her hands were in his hair. I remember thinking it was a strange way to sit together.

At the sound of my voice, Alicia turned her head. My father grunted and then swore as she rose quickly from his lap and came toward me, closing her gown about her. I caught a glimpse of the roundness of breasts and the darkness between her legs.

"What is it, Eduardo?" she asked, kneeling and gathering me to the softness of her gown. "Why the tears?" Her body was warm and musky.

Behind me, Franco said, "I'm sorry, Don Carlos. He just ran past me."

Outside, screams and cries erupted from the other side of the house.

My father glanced out the window, then looked at me and at Franco. "What the devil's going on?" he demanded as he got to his feet. The peculiar state of his penis fascinated me. He took a couple of steps toward us, pulling the bathrobe around his lean, naked body and tying it.

"It's Manuel!" I gasped over Alicia's shoulder, still breathless from my run. "I found him. He's dead!"

Father ran a hand through his mussed hair. "What do you mean, dead? Where'd you find him?"

"In his cottage. In a barrel. He smells awful!"

"God in heaven!"

"His neck's all cut. I was sick."

"Poor boy," Alicia said, still holding and comforting me. "How terrible for you!"

"I better call the authorities," Father said. He thought for a moment, chewing a lip. "Alicia, take Eduard with you and fetch his mother. She should be here to help deal with the police and the servants."

Alicia turned her head toward my father. Her face was drawn. "Where can I find her?"

"She's somewhere along the road that climbs around El Picacho to the north. They went in Mrs Sayed's silver Packard. It should be easy to spot. Franco'll drive you, not the new chauffeur. Go as quickly as possible."

Alicia nodded.

"And you, Eduard, go to your room and wait for your nanny."

Alicia released me, but I remained unmoving, numb.

"Off you go," Father said. There was a weary tone to his voice. "See him to his room, Franco."

As I walked away with Franco, I heard Father say to Alicia, "Talk to Eduard...."

"Come along," Franco ordered, brusquely.

"Soon," Mother says, "there were police all over the place, asking the strangest questions and putting their noses where they shouldn't. They refused, though, to touch the barrel. It was beneath them. And when the doctor and his assistants came from the morgue, they wouldn't touch the barrel either. Said they refused to be responsible for disturbing the evidence. What a business! My husband was very upset."

"So, how did they resolve the stand-off?" Linda asks.

"In a most peculiar way. They argued back and forth until, in the end, the police threw up their hands, and sent for two prisoners from the local jail. Imagine! Two prisoners! Have you ever heard of such a thing? It was the prisoners who finally rolled the barrel through the garden, around to the front and out to the road."

"I remember that," I say, not willing to let Mother off scot-free. "I remember them rolling the barrel as we drove up, you and I and...."

"Drove up? Whatever are you talking about?" She frowns, displeased. Linda frowns as well. I subside. "I was busy with the servants," Mother says and turns back to Linda. "I had my hands full, I can tell you, keeping them from joining the crowd that gathered on the road to see what was happening. It was a noisy crowd, all push and pull, and before the police could stop them, they surrounded the barrel, everyone struggling and elbowing to get a better look. It's hard to believe, but in the confusion, the two prisoners just...slipped away!"

Alicia had sharp eyes. As we drove the rough road around the mountain, El Picacho, which rose to our left, she spotted Helen's Packard, nearly hidden in some trees to the right. She ordered Franco to pull off the road and stop.

On the way, Alicia had told me I should say nothing about what I had seen in her bedroom. "It'd make your mother unhappy and wouldn't be nice for anyone."

But I wasn't interested in what she and Father had been doing. The distorted face of Manuel filled my mind. I could think of nothing else.

As we got out of the car, Alicia told Franco to stay behind. He protested, but, unsure of his authority, complied. Alicia took me by the hand, and we walked to the Packard.

Helen's chauffeur was sitting in the shade near the car. "Which way did they go?" Alicia asked him. She was pleasant, but firm. "We're expected."

The chauffeur hesitated, shrugged and pointed to a trail that led up a hill through scrub. We climbed it quickly.

From the top of the hill, we had a sweeping view of the lower flank of the mountain. Directly before us was a stretch of open ground, downward-sloping, about a kilometre wide. It was grassy, dotted with yellow and pink wildflowers, scrub and a few trees. It was encompassed on three sides by coffee plantations, stretching into the distance, their foliage a rich green.

Mother, Helen and Consuela were a short way down the slope, in a hollow. The two easels were up, paints and palettes nearby, but my mother and Helen weren't painting. They were lying side-by-side on a blanket, naked in the sun, their clothes piled next to them. Mother was on her stomach, and Helen on her back, nipples large on her small breasts. Mother's arm lay across Helen's belly, hand absently stroking flank. Their bodies were copper. Nearby, in the shade of a stunted tree, sat Consuela, reading. She wore a simple dress and one of Mother's sun hats. She could never understand why people would want to darken themselves.

As soon as I saw them, I struggled free of Alicia's hand and dashed ahead, thinking only of my news. At the sound of my approach, Mother and Helen sat up abruptly and pulled on their painter's smocks. They were buttoning them as I ran up and breathlessly told them about Manuel.

"How awful," said Mother. Her distress was vague. Consuela, on the other hand, appeared stricken.

Alicia, coming up behind me, told Mother that my father needed her to come right away, that everything was in an uproar. The car was waiting for her at the roadside.

Mother looked through Alicia for a moment, and then instructed her to take me back to the car. She said she'd join us shortly.

"Why aren't you and Helen wearing anything?" I asked Mother.

She exchanged a glance with Helen. "Run along now," she said to me.

"When they couldn't find the prisoners," Mother says, "the police were obliged to send for a second pair, who extracted the body from the barrel. That was not a pleasant scene, I can assure you. Everyone held handkerchiefs to their noses, and the prisoners loaded the body into the ambulance, and that, I'm afraid, was the end of Manuel."

"Did they ever find out who murdered him?" Linda asks.

"Never," Mother replies. "Perhaps the servants knew something, but they didn't speak up."

"Servants know better than to say all they know," Consuela remarks. Her expression is unreadable. She gets up to clear the table for dessert. "You have an astonishing memory, Aunt Mary. You remember things I can't at all."

"You were young," Mother says. She smiles to herself, satisfied with her story.

I finally understand what she's doing. She's cutting away

the untamed undergrowth in her life and replacing it with orderly beds of flowers, even if the colours are somewhat macabre. In a way, she's trying to recreate a state of blamelessness, and so complete the cycle of her life. She's hoping Linda, and ultimately Consuela and me, will accept this changed landscape, or at least allow her to. It's understandable, I suppose. After all, there are parts of my own life I wouldn't mind revising.

After Manuel's death, so much changed that I felt my world was being turned on its head. First, my nanny disappeared overnight, without explanation. Franco followed. My father moved into a bedroom of his own, and, within a month, Helen departed for a lengthy visit with relatives in Australia. Even Pablo vanished. He was found dead one morning, or so I was told. The servants whispered among themselves, and I heard Consuela's name, but they fell silent when I drew near. As for me, I was further burdened with tutors for several months before being shipped off to boarding-school.

One night, about a month after Manuel's death, I couldn't sleep, so I stole out onto the terrace. The moon was full, and the terrace was tinted by a pale green luminescence. I was surprised to find Consuela there, standing at the edge of the flagstones and looking out over the garden in the direction of Manuel's cottage. I went and stood beside her and took her hand. Tears streaked her face.

"Why are you crying?" I asked. "Is it because he can't give you flowers anymore?"

"Because of that," she said, "and because...I'm confused about things...about your mother...." She fell silent.

"I miss Manuel," I said.

Consuela knelt and took me in her arms and hugged me. It was a rare display of affection. "You loved him, didn't you?"

"Yes."

"So did I. He was such a kind man—if not always wise. I wish I'd loved him more...or less. Either way, he might not have...." She couldn't finish. "Remember him for both of us," she said, and got up and ran into the house.

Then, during this same period, there came a morning when I got tired of being hectored by my German tutor and escaped to the garden. I was seeking solace, but the garden wasn't the refuge it had been. The newly hired gardener was there. He glared when he saw me. We'd never be friends.

I wandered among the flowerbeds, absently reached out and scooped a bee in my hand.

"Watch out, you little fool!" the gardener exclaimed. "It'll hurt you!" A dark doubt slipped into my mind. The bee promptly stung me. "You asked for it!" the gardener said, but I pretended the sting didn't hurt.

I returned to the house, fighting back tears. The tears were less for the pain than for the way everything had changed. There was so much I didn't understand, and I remember being angry that even the bees weren't the same. I was finished with bees.

"Edward!" Linda says. "You're gathering wool."

"I'm sorry. Did I miss something?"

"Your mother...."

"I was just saying, Edward, how much you enjoyed boarding-school, and what a world of good it did you."

Well, now. It seems Mother's not yet done with rearranging her garden.

Horse from Persia

THE LAST-MINUTE LAMENT OF ALEXANDER J. HARE

Christian Petersen

December 9th, 1879

The Kamloops posse, led by Justice of the Peace John Clapperton, had by now learned of the outlaws' whereabouts and converged on the cabin they occupied. Notes were exchanged. On the scrap of paper, Clapperton read:

> *"Mr. Clapperton,*
> *Sir—*
> *The Boys say they will not surrender, and so you can burn the house a thousand times over.*
> *Alexr. J. Hare.*
> *I wish to know what you all have against me. If you have anything, please let me know what it is.*
> *A.H."*

After two days without food or water the gang surrendered.

January 31st, 1881

The condemned men were attended early by their spiritual advisors, Reverend Father Horris and two other priests. They proceeded to the place of execution, mounted the scaffold, and were each given the opportunity to address the townspeople assembled. Hare stood at the west end, and was the last to speak.

He said: I forgive everyone and thank everyone for their kindness...that is, the kindness pointed out to me earlier this morning by the good priest. What's more I'd like to thank you all for coming out, for maybe rushing your breakfasts to be here, to hear my last words, and see me hang. Never imagined I'd die in the morning.... A bit chilly, don't you find? Looking at me, as I stand here, you good people may not believe I've paid death much thought. But I have. I don't deny, I did carve Constable's face with my skinner knife. As he cried and sputtered, I laughed even 'cause it sounded funny, his voice running for its life, stronger than his body—till Archie shot him. Such a thing's not easy to forget. Death seems a sudden quiet surprise.... It is this time, this morning, my only chance in life to speak—too much to say—like panic in a fistfight, them or you, you got to control that shivery chill to save yourself. And it—it's tough finding words. Don't know many, but Ma tried to teach me. Though whatever use she had in mind, for me to make of words, was harder still to learn. What I have to say now is all that comes of her hope. It struck me in that cabin, where the posse had us trapped— the Boys, cursing in whispers, they told me to write a note for Clapperton, for they know even less than I.... I remember Ma's voice, years ago, telling about Jonah, about blind Samson pulling them pillars down, and how the first beast was like a lion, and the second like a calf. Leather Bible closed soft in her hands, hands made tough in spots from work, the skin of her arms against my face was more tender. Sometimes I waked later, hearing wind, and some nights Ma's cries. Though it was clearly her voice, it was not the voice I knew, and alone I recalled to myself how the third beast had a face as a man. Ma's hands shiny with grease at breakfast, working under coal-oil light. Pa rolling tobacco, smoking, silent, or declaring: *Them wolves is killin' the cows, and I'm gonna kill me some goddamn wolves!* Though the cattle were mostly starved in the first place, as a result of Pa's own bitter laziness. His land was too high and stony to grow much hay, up against the iron rusty ridges north of Kamloops. From the back porch we looked out to a scowling face of such rock, and windstorms swooped along against the cliff, bringing brief rains in spring, sometimes lickety-split out of blue sky, and more dust, hail, snow. Light, too, Ma showed me, bending, touching my hair and pointing with her arm, the light racing in those different storms. Smoke blackened the logs of the cabin inside, like Pa's own madness, darker, crazier as seasons passed, and fit to kill me once I turned fifteen, less than four years back.... That trapper's cabin down by Copper Slough, hid in a stand of swamp spruce where the raggedy moss hung, twisted in breezes, that's where I met up with the Boys. Plenty of liquor to go around. Sick from it, lying swirling beneath witch trees, and far off stars. Owls like spirits passing over. And at the edge of this dark sometimes again came Ma's whisper: till I'd crawl after it, scrape myself in the brush, crawl through moonwhite sharp swampgrass, till mud sucked my fingers at the edge of the shimmery still water. While the Boys threw knives in the cabin. Out there, far from here or any town, a secret thing grew in me, lived and wriggled like pain in my body so I feared it, yet wanted it more. And lying on my back under the powerful weight of myself, I was sure I'd die some other *night* in the future, and felt strange comfort. Wasn't even true, what I was sure of. For here I stand, this morning—oh—pardon my panic, every thought brings some other and all in a rush it's hard to sort their order out.... Days later, riding through the settlement on a stolen horse the Boys loaned me, old neighbours stared at me like a stranger. Which struck me silly then. I laughed hard, half-drunk in the saddle, sweaty from sun. And we carried on.... We rode north. It was the summer before last, before any of the murdering, we worked a stretch on a ranch near Williams Lake. This ranch was owned by a man named Doc English, called so for his way with horses. He loved horses. He talked mostly to me, it seemed, as the Boys would often not answer when talked to. Doc seemed to me a fair man, though most mindful of his own share of what's fair, as any smart man is. So this was our job, he said, to build some Russell fence across his land because Doc believed certain folks were not recognizing what was his, or what was theirs. And we dragged jack-pines with our ponies, and slung these poles together in teepees with wire, and it went on and on, and we talked some as we worked till we figured out this work would never end if we gave in to it, goddamn it, how we hated building fence. Put in nine days, asked Doc for our pay. This decision of ours did not seem to shock Doc English. But he had something more to say. 'Cause he'd seen Archie ride, knew Archie could ride a grizzly if you'd ever get a saddle on one, so he asked: Son, how would you like to make this much money again, but only in a few minutes? See, Doc had a running horse which he wanted to race, a wonder of a horse it was too. What the hell, says Archie. Then we left the ranch, took what money we had, got good and drunk in town. A couple of days before the race Doc met up with me and Archie, asked us over to the eating house. He bought us a meal. He told us about the miracle horse, how its bloodline came direct from Persia, how it seemed to fly more than run. From his talk I saw the life of this horse was the precious free part of Doc's life also. Then a pretty girl brought us some stew and biscuits. And she brought a silence over our table. Archie asked her, and she said her name was Martha. Though she spoke quiet, lean-ing slightly over the table, I clearly heard her voice and it put a sort of spell on me, like music. Archie was bold as ever. I worried she thought us rude, because I desired to talk with her afterward, alone. She was uncommonly pretty, her hair dark as coffee, with eyes to match, and her mouth had a strong kind look.... Anyhow, what Doc didn't know yet was that Archie had also parleyed with McDougall, owner of the other horse to run. Archie figured to take money from them both, you see. This did not seem alto-gether a wise plan, in my mind. However I stayed quiet, while Doc and Archie talked over the race. I watched Martha while she served other tables. My notions were foolish, but tender. If Archie tried any evil with her, I swore I'd kill him. So we ate, and Doc rambled on, till finally Archie went out back to piss. And while he was gone Doc turned more serious, looked straight at me and said I seemed awful quiet. Martha stopped at our table with the coffee pot, and as she poured it in our mugs I wanted to thank her, but my breath locked in my chest, and I could not. After she walked away, Doc he stared deeper into my eyes, and though I said nothing I believe it was then he guessed mean nature was at work.... We camped outside town, and waited two days till the race. Never did talk with Martha. She was fine, too fine for me I knew, and I felt a bit lost, much more alone then like a scared child. And I began to see how, riding with the Boys, I'd left someplace, and now could not go back. Like a rank horse that breaks loose or leaps a fence, but then wonders where he's going, now that he's on his own. What did I want? It seemed already too late for my answer to make any difference, so there came a tiny hint of doom in my mind.... The morning of the race was sunny as any I've seen, and the beautiful horses were nervous and snorting, for they knew something was up, and that they were at centre of it. Doc was cheery, even a bit loud, telling folks again how the bloodline of his horse came direct from Persia, and how it'd run so fast that any-one who rode it had better tie their own belt to the saddle horn or risk gettin' left behind. It was true enough that the colt was an awful fine creature. Its coat was dappled dun, with coal black mane and tail, a white star was on its fore-head, and its face made you think it had a mind least as good as your own, like it was some kind of horse out of the Bible. Lots of people gathered for the race. It was a clean morning full with excitement. And I remember that I briefly wished to have been there, as others seemed to be, without many burdens on my Soul, free from the icy tip of worry digging inside me. For Ma often told me how our Time is a gift and in me had started a fear I was wasting what was given me. But, for causes I can't explain, I was more scared to accept it. So on any track I might take, fear stalked me, and I truly wished that somehow I could escape from it.... Doc was a man who could sort things out. Folks said he'd crossed the Frontier, nearly been scalped, had been through worse fixes than most people dream of. While he employed us, on a couple of afternoons when work was

done for the day, he told stories—he told one about the
Oregon trail, which he travelled as a boy, one day he and
his Pa had stayed behind the wagon train, to pick berries
for pie, and they was seen by a war party and got chased, it
was godawful-hell-for-leather for miles, till the wagons
came in sight, and even then one of them braves put an ar-
row into the gut of Doc's pony, and the thing died right out
from under him. Oh he liked to talk, how some men do,
and he had many other stories. Some that weren't so exciting at the time—but I dearly wish I could recall them now
only to add to my own, and to make you listen, longer....
Anyhow, during the two days prior to the horse race he had
asked particular people in the settlement a few questions,
and pretty quick figured out Archie's secret greedy plan.
McDougall and his pals were snickering into their fists, and
so Doc let them enjoy the joke for a bit. Finally the man in
charge of the race shouted out that it was time. Archie
swung into the saddle. The sun shone down, rich as new
money. The blessed horse from Persia pranced, every step
closer to the starting line, all set to run. The horse knew
Doc, of course, and so it stood calm when Doc approached
it. It appeared Doc was gonna give a bit of last second ad-
vice. Then he reached up, took hold of Archie's shirt,
yanked him right out of the saddle and dropped him on
the ground. *Young scoundrel!* he hollered, *You'll ride no horse
of mine!* But now came the thing Doc didn't know, or
McDougall either most likely, and that was Archie's hidden
derringer out from his pants aimed straight at Doc's gut.
There was a moment of awful quiet, or only half a moment
maybe, with the stubby silver barrel shining—before another man struck down his arm. Others fell on Archie, and
took the gun away. During this confusion the horse jumped
a few steps to the side. And I looked away from the men
fighting and yelling, to the beautiful horse. I wished might-
ily that I could climb up on that horse and escape the sorrowful puzzle my days had become. For if it's true Time is
a gift, mine was not altogether pleasant—and I ask that
fact be noted beside my name in the Book of Life. Sure, all
people are born on this Earth, and maybe that itself is a

kind of gift, but we're not all born to the same world, and cruel differences on Earth between the worlds of men can make our Time here a heavy gift to bear, so it seems to me. This idea has not only rushed into my head this morning, as you might think and maybe snicker, when I confess I'm inclined to speak every strange and no-account idea I ever had to delay the stretching of my neck—my silence—the quiet surprise. No!.... Oh, my memory rushes back to the morning of the race, to the sight of the miracle horse in the sunlight, his dun coat shining, his noble head and eyes and bloodline from Persia. And if only I had that horse and fine Martha, my heart cried to my mind, I could get away! For once to the woman were given two wings of a great eagle, that she might fly into the wilderness, and be nourished there and safe from the face of the serpent. I swore if ever I were free in that way I would accept the gift of Time, the life given me. I recall Ma's hand on my hair, her bending close to me, her arm pointing to light in the storms along the ridge, her voice.... As it was, because of Archie's sneaky plan, the townspeople turned unfriendly and ran the Boys and me clean out of that town. Further down the trail, we heard that Doc's horse had easily won that race. This news did not surprise me, but caused some pain in my heart because I remembered fine Martha, and the dun colt dancing in sunlight. I have not forgotten, though many times I've wished to, have even told my mind not to think of it. I remember all these moments I speak of. And if different lives, different times, were put before me now to choose, like gifts on a table, 'course I would choose the finest, and never the fearsome sort I've had.... I cannot speak for you all, and don't claim to. Only for myself.... Hanging is a kindness that's somewhat hard for me to understand, and harder to thank you for and smile. But I'm grateful to you for hearing me out this morning, my only chance to speak, while I await the last surprise.... Ah, surely there's plenty more to say.... If you give me only another minute I will think of it....

The Hangman then adjusted the ropes, commencing with Hare; the signal was given by the Sheriff, and the doomed men fell.

The Love of a Good Woman

Alice Munro

For the last couple of decades, there has been a museum in Walley, dedicated to preserving photos and butter churns and horse harnesses and an old dentist's chair and a cumbersome apple peeler and such curiosities as the pretty little porcelain-and-glass insulators that were used on telegraph poles. Also there is a red box, which has the letters "D.M. Willens, Optometrist," printed on it, and a note beside it, saying, "This box of optometrist's instruments though not very old has considerable local significance, since it belonged to Mr. D.M. Willens, who drowned in the Peregrine River, 1951. It escaped the catastrophe and was found, presumably by the anonymous donor, who dispatched it to be a feature of our collection."

The ophthalmoscope could make you think of a snowman. The top part, that is—the part that's fastened onto the hollow handle. A large disk, with a smaller disk on top. In the large disk a hole to look through, as the various lenses are moved. The handle is heavy because the batteries are still inside. If you took the batteries out and put in the rod that is provided, with a disk on either end, you could plug in an electric cord. But it might have been necessary to use the instrument in places where there wasn't any electricity.

The retinoscope looks more complicated. Underneath the round forehead clamp is something like an elf's head, with a round flat face and a pointed metal cap. This is tilted at a 45° angle to a slim column, and out of the top of the column a tiny light is supposed to shine. The flat face is made of glass and is a dark sort of mirror.

Everything is black, but that is only paint. In some places where the optometrist's hand must have rubbed most often, the paint has disappeared and you can see a patch of shiny silver metal.

I. JUTLAND

This place was called Jutland. There had been a mill once, and some kind of small settlement, but that had all gone by the end of the last century, and the place had never amounted to much at any time. Many people believed that it had been named in honour of the famous sea battle fought during the First World War, but actually everything had been in ruins years before that battle ever took place.

The three boys who came out here on a Saturday morning early in the spring of 1951 believed, as most children did, that the name came from the old wooden planks that jutted out of the earth of the riverbank and from the other straight thick boards that stood up in the nearby water, making an uneven palisade. (These were in fact the remains of a dam, built before the days of cement.) The planks and a heap of foundation stones and a lilac bush and some huge apple trees deformed by black knot and the shallow ditch of the millrace that filled up with nettles every summer were the only other signs of what had been here before.

There was a road, or a track, coming back from the township road, but it had never been gravelled, and appeared on the maps only as a dotted line, a road allowance. It was used quite a bit in the summer by people driving to the river to swim or at night by couples looking for a place to park. The turnaround spot came before you got to the ditch, but the whole area was so overrun by nettles, and cow parsnip, and woody wild hemlock in a wet year, that cars would sometimes have to back out all the way to the proper road.

The car tracks to the water's edge on that spring morning were easy to spot but were not taken notice of by these boys, who were thinking only about swimming. At least, they would call it swimming; they would go back to town and say that they had been swimming at Jutland before the snow was off the ground.

It was colder here upstream than on the river flats close to the town. There was not a leaf out yet on the riverbank trees—the only green you saw was from patches of leeks on the ground and marsh marigolds fresh as spinach, spread along any little stream that gullied its way down to the river. And on the opposite bank under some cedars they saw what they were especially looking for—a long, low, stubborn snowbank, grey as stones.

Not off the ground.

So they would jump into the water and feel the cold hit them like ice daggers. Ice daggers shooting up behind their eyes and jabbing the tops of their skulls from the inside. Then they would move their arms and legs a few times and haul themselves out, quaking and letting their teeth rattle; they would push their numb limbs into their clothes and feel the painful recapture of their bodies by their startled blood and the relief of making their brag true.

The tracks that they didn't notice came right through the ditch—in which there was nothing growing now, there was only the flat dead straw-coloured grass of the year before. Through the ditch and into the river without trying to turn around. The boys tramped over them. But by this time they were close enough to the water to have had their attention caught by something more extraordinary than car tracks.

There was a pale-blue shine to the water that was not a reflection of sky. It was a whole car, down in the pond on a slant, the front wheels and the nose of it poking into the mud on the bottom, and the bump of the trunk nearly breaking the surface. Light blue was in those days an unusual colour for a car, and its bulgy shape was unusual, too. They knew it right away. The little English car, the Austin, the only one of its kind surely in the whole county. It belonged to Mr. Willens, the optometrist. He looked like a cartoon character when he drove it, because he was a short but thick man, with heavy shoulders and a large head. He always seemed to be crammed into his little car as if it were a bursting suit of clothes.

The car had a panel in its roof, which Mr. Willens opened in warm weather. It was open now. They could not see very well what was inside. The colour of the car made its shape plain in the water, but the water was really not very clear, and it obscured what was not so bright. The boys squatted down on the bank, then lay on their stomachs and pushed their heads out like turtles, trying to see. There was something dark and furry, something like a big animal tail, pushed up through the hole in the roof and moving idly in the water. This was shortly seen to be an arm, covered by the sleeve of a dark jacket of some heavy and hairy material. It seemed that inside the car a man's body—it had to be the body of Mr. Willens—had got into a peculiar position. The force of the water—for even in the millpond there was a good deal of force in the water at this time of year—must have somehow lifted him from the seat and pushed him about, so that one shoulder was up near the car roof and one arm had got free. His head must have been shoved down against the driver's door and window. One front wheel was stuck deeper in the river bottom than the other, which meant that the car was on a slant from side to side as well as back to front. The window in fact must be open and the head sticking out for the body to be lodged in that position. But they could not get to see that. They could picture Mr. Willens' face as they knew it—a big square face, which often wore a theatrical sort of frown but was never seriously intimidating. His thin crinkly hair was reddish or brassy on top, and combed diagonally over his forehead. His eyebrows were darker than his hair, thick and fuzzy like caterpillars stuck above his eyes. This was a face already grotesque to them, in the way that many adult faces were, and they were not afraid to see it drowned. But all they got to see was that arm and his pale hand. They could see the hand quite plain once they got used to looking through the water. It rode there tremulously and irresolutely, like a feather, though it looked as solid as dough. And as ordinary, once you got used to its being there at all. The fingernails were all like neat little faces, with their intelligent everyday look of greeting, their sensible disowning of their circumstances.

"Son of a gun," these boys said. With gathering energy and a tone of deepening respect, even of gratitude. "*Son of a gun*."

It was their first time out this year. First, they had come across the bridge over the Peregrine River, the single-lane double-span bridge known locally as Hell's Gate or the Death Trap—though the danger had really more to do with the sharp turn the road took at the south end of it than with the bridge itself.

There was a regular walkway for pedestrians, but they didn't use it. They never remembered using it. Perhaps years ago, when they were so young as to be held by the hand. But that time had vanished for them; they refused to recognize it even if they were shown the evidence in snapshots or forced to listen to it in family conversation.

They walked now along the iron shelf that ran on the opposite side of the bridge from the walkway. It was about eight inches wide and a foot or so above the bridge floor. The Peregrine River was rushing the winter load of ice and snow, now melted, out into Lake Huron. It was barely back within its banks after the yearly flood that turned the flats into a lake and tore out the young trees and bashed any boat or hut within its reach. With the runoff from the fields muddying the water and the pale sunlight on its surface, the water looked like butterscotch pudding on the boil. But if you fell into it it would freeze your blood and fling you out into the lake, if it didn't brain you against the buttresses first.

Cars honked at them—a warning or a reproof—but they paid no attention. They proceeded single file, as self-possessed as sleepwalkers. Then, at the north end of the bridge, they cut down to the flats, locating the paths they remembered from the year before. The flood had been so recent that these paths were not easy to follow. You had to kick your way through beaten-down brush and jump from one hummock of mud-plastered grass to another. Sometimes they jumped carelessly and landed in mud or pools of leftover floodwater, and once their feet were wet they gave up caring where they landed. They squelched through the mud and splashed in the pools so that the water came in over the tops of their rubber boots. The wind was warm; it was pulling the clouds apart into threads of old wool, and the gulls and crows were quarrelling and diving over the river. Buzzards were circling over them, on the high lookout; the robins had just returned, and the red-winged blackbirds were darting in pairs, striking bright on your eyes as if they had been dipped in paint.

"Should've brought a twenty-two."

"Should've brought a twelve-gauge."

They were too old to raise sticks and make shooting noises. They spoke with casual regret, as if guns were readily available to them.

They climbed up the north banks to a place where there was bare sand. Turtles were supposed to lay their eggs in this sand. It was too early yet for that to happen, and in fact the story of turtle eggs dated from years back—none of these boys had ever seen any. But they kicked and stomped the sand, just in case. Then they looked around for the place where last year one of them, in company with another boy, had found a cow's hipbone, carried off by the flood from some slaughter pile. The river could be counted on every year to sweep off and deposit elsewhere a good number of surprising or cumbersome or bizarre or homely objects. Rolls of wire, an intact set of steps, a bent shovel, a corn kettle. The hipbone had been found caught on the branch of a sumac—which seemed proper, because all those smooth branches were like cow horns or deer antlers, some with rusty cone tips. They crashed around for some time—Cece Ferns showed them the exact branch—but they found nothing.

It was Cece Ferns and Ralph Diller who had made that find, and when asked where it was at present Cece Ferns said, "Ralph took it." The two boys who were with him now—Jimmy Box and Bud Salter—knew why that would have to be. Cece could never take anything home unless it was of a size to be easily concealed from his father.

They talked of more useful finds that might be made or had been made in past years. Fence rails could be used to build a raft, pieces of stray lumber could be collected for a planned shack or boat. Real luck would be to get hold of some loose muskrat traps. Then you could go into business. You could pick up enough lumber for stretching boards and steal the knives for skinning. They spoke of taking over an empty shed they knew of, in the blind alley behind what used to be the livery barn. There was a padlock on it, but you could probably get in through the window, taking the boards off it at night and replacing them at daybreak. You could take a flashlight to work by. No—a lantern. You could skin the muskrats and stretch the pelts and sell them for a lot of money.

This project became so real to them that they started to worry about leaving valuable pelts in the shed all day. One of them would have to stand watch while the others went out on the traplines. (Nobody mentioned school.)

This was the way they talked when they got clear of town. They talked as if they were free—or almost free— agents, as if they didn't go to school or live with families or suffer any of the indignities put on them because of their age. Also, as if the countryside and other people's establishments would provide them with all they needed for their undertakings and adventures, with only the smallest risk and effort on their part.

Another change in their conversation out here was that they practically gave up using names. They didn't use each other's real names much anyway—not even family nicknames such as Bud. But at school nearly everyone had another name, some of these having to do with the way people looked or talked, like Goggle or Jabber, and some, like Sorearse and Chickenfucker, having to do with incidents real or fabulous in the lives of those named, or in the lives— such names were handed down for decades—of their brothers, fathers or uncles. These were the names they let go of when they were out in the bush or on the river flats. If they had to get one another's attention, all they said was "Hey." Even the use of names that were outrageous and obscene and that grownups supposedly never heard would have spoiled a sense they had at these times, of taking each other's looks, habits, family and personal history entirely for granted.

And yet they hardly thought of each other as friends. They would never have designated someone as a best friend or a next-best friend, or joggled people around in these positions, the way girls did. Any one of at least a dozen boys could have been substituted for any one of these three, and accepted by the others in exactly the same way. Most members of that company were between nine and twelve years old, too old to be bound by yards and neighbourhoods but too young to have jobs—even jobs sweeping the sidewalk in front of stores or delivering groceries by bicycle. Most of them lived in the north end of town, which meant that they would be expected to get a job of that sort as soon as they were old enough, and that none of them would ever be sent away to Appleby or to Upper Canada College. And none of them lived in a shack or had a relative in jail. Just the same, there were notable differences as to how they lived at home and what was expected of them in life. But these differences dropped away as soon as they were out of sight of the county jail and the grain elevator and the church steeples and out of range of the chimes of the courthouse clock.

On their way back they walked fast. Sometimes they trotted but did not run. Jumping, dallying, splashing were all abandoned, and the noises they'd made on their way out, the hoots and howls, were put aside as well. Any windfall of the flood was taken note of but passed by. In fact they made their way as adults would do, at a fairly steady speed and by the most reasonable route, with the weight on them of where they had to go and what had to be done next. They had something close in front of them, a picture in front of their eyes that came between them and the world, which was exactly the thing most adults seemed to have. The pond, the car, the arm, the hand. They had some idea that when they got to a certain spot they would start to shout. They would come into town yelling and waving their news around them and everybody would be stock still, taking it in.

They crossed the bridge the same way as always, on the shelf. But they had no sense of risk or courage or nonchalance. They might as well have taken the walkway.

Instead of following the sharp-turning road from which you could reach both the harbour and the square, they climbed straight up the bank on a path that came out near the railway sheds. The clock played its quarter-after chimes. A quarter after twelve.

This was the time when people were walking home for dinner. People from offices had the afternoon off. But people who worked in stores were getting only their customary hour—the stores stayed open till ten or eleven o'clock on Saturday night.

Most people were going home to a hot, filling meal. Pork chops, or sausages, or boiled beef, or cottage roll. Potatoes for certain, mashed or fried; winter-stored root vegetables or cabbage or creamed onions. (A few housewives, richer or more feckless, might have opened a tin of peas or butter beans.) Bread, muffins, preserves, pie. Even those people who didn't have a home to go to, or who for some reason didn't want to go there, would be sitting down to much the same sort of food at the Duke of Cumberland, or the Merchants' Hotel, or for less money behind the foggy windows of Shervill's Dairy Bar.

Those walking home were mostly men. The women were already there—they were there all the time. But some women of middle age who worked in stores or offices for a reason that was not their fault—dead husbands or sick husbands or never any husband at all—were friends of the boys' mothers, and they called out greetings even across the street (it was worst for Bud Salter, whom they called Buddy) in a certain amused or sprightly way that brought to mind all they knew of family matters, of distant infancies.

Men didn't bother greeting boys by name, even if they knew them well. They called them "boys" or "young fellows" or, occasionally, "sirs."

"Good day to you, sirs."

"You boys going straight home now?"

"What monkey business you young fellows been up to this morning?"

All these greetings had a degree of jocularity, but there were differences. The men who said "young fellows" were better disposed—or wished to seem better disposed—than the ones who said "boys." "Boys" could be the signal that a telling off was to follow, for offenses that could be either vague or specific. "Young fellows" indicated that the speaker had once been young himself. "Sirs" was outright mockery and disparagement but didn't open the way to any scolding, because the person who said that could not be bothered.

When answering, the boys didn't look up past any lady's purse or any man's Adam's apple. They said "Hullo" clearly, because there might be some kind of trouble if you didn't, and in answer to queries they said "Yessir" and "Nosir" and "Nothing much." Even on this day, such voices speaking to them caused some alarm and confusion, and they replied with the usual reticence.

At a certain corner they had to separate. Cece Ferns, always the most anxious about getting home, pulled away first. He said, "See you after dinner."

Bud Salter said, "Yeah. We got to go downtown then."

This meant, as they all understood, "downtown to the Police Office." It seemed that without needing to consult each other they had taken up a new plan of operation, a soberer way of telling their news. But it wasn't clearly said that they wouldn't be telling anything at home. There wasn't any good reason why Bud Salter or Jimmy Box couldn't have done that.

Cece Ferns never told anything at home.

Cece Ferns was an only child. His parents were older than most boys' parents, or perhaps they only seemed older, because of the disabling life they lived together. When he got away from the other boys, Cece started to trot, as he usually did for the last block home. This was not because he was eager to get there or because he thought he could make anything better when he did. It may have been to make the time pass quickly, because the last block had to be full of apprehension.

His mother was in the kitchen. Good. She was out of bed though still in her wrapper. His father wasn't there, and that was good, too. His father worked at the grain elevator and got Saturday afternoon off, and if he wasn't home by now it was likely that he had gone straight to the Cumberland. That meant it would be late in the day before they had to deal with him.

Cece's father's name was Cece Ferns, too. It was a well-known and generally an affectionately known name in Walley, and somebody telling a story even 30 or 40 years later would take it for granted that everybody would know it was the father who was being talked about, not the son. If a person relatively new in town said, "That doesn't sound like Cece," he would be told that nobody meant *that* Cece.

"Not him, we're talking about his old man."

They talked about the time Cece Ferns went to the hospital—or was taken there—with pneumonia, or some other desperate thing, and the nurses wrapped him in wet towels or sheets to get the fever down. The fever sweated out of him, and all the towels and sheets turned brown. It was the nicotine in him. The nurses had never seen anything like it. Cece was delighted. He claimed to have been smoking tobacco and drinking alcohol since he was ten years old.

And the time he went to church. It was hard to imagine why, but it was the Baptist church, and his wife was a Baptist, so perhaps he went to please her, though that was even harder to imagine. They were serving Communion the Sunday he went, and in the Baptist Church the bread is bread but the wine is grape juice. "What's this?" cried Cece Ferns aloud. "If this is the blood of the Lamb then He must've been pretty damn anemic."

Preparations for the noon meal were under way in the

Fernses' kitchen. A loaf of sliced bread was sitting on the table and a can of diced beets had been opened. A few slices of bologna had been fried—before the eggs, though they should have been done after—and were being kept slightly warm on top of the stove. And now Cece's mother had started the eggs. She was bending over the stove with the egg lifter in one hand and the other hand pressed to her stomach, cradling a pain.

Cece took the egg lifter out of her hand and turned down the electric heat, which was way too high. He had to hold the pan off the burner while the burner cooled down, in order to keep the egg whites from getting too tough or burning at the edges. He hadn't been in time to wipe out the old grease and plop a bit of fresh lard in the pan. His mother never wiped out the old grease, just let it sit from one meal to the next and put in a bit of lard when she had to.

When the heat was more to his liking, he put the pan down and coaxed the lacy edges of the eggs into tidy circles. He found a clean spoon and dribbled a little hot fat over the yokes to set them. He and his mother liked their eggs cooked this way, but his mother often couldn't manage it right. His father liked his eggs turned over and flattened out like pancakes, cooked hard as shoe leather and blackened with pepper. Cece could cook them the way he wanted, too.

None of the other boys knew how practiced he was in the kitchen—just as none of them knew about the hiding place he had made outside the house in the blind corner past the dining-room window, behind the Japanese barberry.

His mother sat in the chair by the window while he was finishing up the eggs. She kept an eye on the street. There was still a chance that his father would come home for something to eat. He might not be drunk yet. But the way he behaved didn't always depend on how drunk he was. If he came into the kitchen now he might tell Cece to make him some eggs, too. Then he might ask him where his apron was and say that he would make some fellow a dandy wife. That would be how he'd behave if he was in a good mood. In another sort of mood he would start off by staring at Cece in a certain way—that is, with an exaggerated, absurdly threatening expression—and telling him he better watch out.

"Smart bugger, aren't you? Well, all I got to say to you is, better watch out."

Then if Cece looked back at him, or maybe if he didn't look back, or if he dropped the egg lifter or set it down with a clatter—or even if he was sliding around being extra cautious about not dropping anything and not making a noise—his father was apt to start showing his teeth and snarling like a dog. It would have been ridiculous—it was ridiculous—except that he meant business. A minute later the food and the dishes might be on the floor and the chairs or the table overturned and he might be chasing Cece around the room yelling how he was going to get him this time, flatten his face on the hot burner, how would he like that? You would be certain he'd gone crazy. But if at this moment a knock came at the door—if a friend of his arrived, say, to pick him up—his face would reassemble itself in no time and he would open the door and call out the friend's name in a loud bantering voice.

"I'll be with you in two shakes. I'd ask you in, but the wife's been pitching the dishes around again."

He didn't intend this to be believed. He said such things in order to turn whatever happened in his house into a joke.

Cece's mother asked him if the weather was warming up and where he had been that morning.

"Yeah," he said, and, "Out on the flats."

She said that she'd thought she could smell the wind on him.

"You know what I'm going to do right after we eat?" she said. "I'm going to take a hot-water bottle and go right back to bed and maybe I'll get my strength back and feel like doing something."

That was what she nearly always said she was going to do, but she always announced it as if it were an idea that had just occurred to her, a hopeful decision.

Bud Salter had two older sisters who never did anything useful unless his mother made them. And they never confined their hair arranging, nail polishing, shoe cleaning, making up, or even dressing activities to their bedrooms or the bathroom. They spread their combs and curlers and face powder and nail polish and shoe polish all over the house. Also they loaded every chair back with their newly ironed dresses and blouses and spread out their drying sweaters on towels on every clear space of floor. (Then they screamed at you if you walked near them.) They stationed themselves in front of various mirrors—the mirror in the hall coat-stand, the mirror in the dining-room buffet and the mirror beside the kitchen door with the shelf underneath always loaded with safety pins, bobby pins, pennies, buttons, bits of pencils. Sometimes one of them would stand in front of a mirror for twenty minutes or so, checking herself from various angles, inspecting her teeth and pulling her hair back then shaking it forward. Then she would walk away apparently satisfied or at least finished—but only as far as the next room, the next mirror, where she would begin all over again just as if she had been delivered a new head.

Right now his older sister, the one who was supposed to be good-looking, was taking the pins out of her hair in front of the kitchen mirror. Her head was covered with shiny curls like snails. His other sister, on orders from his mother, was mashing the potatoes. His five-year-old brother was sitting in place at the table, banging his knife and fork up and down and yelling, "Want some service. Want some service."

He got that from their father, who did it for a joke.

Bud passed by his brother's chair and said quietly, "Look. She's putting lumps in the mashed potatoes again."

He had his brother convinced that lumps were something you added, like raisins to rice pudding, from a supply in the cupboard.

His brother stopped chanting and began complaining.

"I won't eat none if she puts in lumps. Mama, I won't eat none if she puts lumps."

"Oh, don't be silly," Bud's mother said. She was frying

apple slices and onion rings with the pork chops. "Quit whining like a baby."

"It was Bud got him started," the older sister said. "Bud went and told him she was putting lumps in. Bud always tells him that and he doesn't know any better."

"Bud ought to get his face smashed," said Doris, the sister who was mashing the potatoes. She didn't always say such things idly—she had once left a claw scar down the side of Bud's cheek.

Bud went over to the dresser, where there was a rhubarb pie cooling. He took a fork and began carefully, secretly prying at it, letting out delicious steam, a delicate smell of cinnamon. He was trying to open one of the vents in the top of it so that he could get a taste of the filling. His brother saw what he was doing but was too scared to say anything. His brother was spoiled and was defended by his sisters all the time—Bud was the only person in the house he respected.

"Want some service," he repeated, speaking now in a thoughtful undertone.

Doris came over to the dresser to get the bowl for the mashed potatoes. Bud made an incautious movement, and part of the top crust caved in.

"So now he's wrecking the pie," Doris said. "Mama—he's wrecking your pie."

"Shut your damn mouth," Bud said.

"Leave that pie alone," said Bud's mother with a practiced, almost serene severity. "Stop swearing. Stop tattletelling. Grow up."

Jimmy Box sat down to dinner at a crowded table. He and his father and his mother and his four-year-old and six-year-old sisters lived in his grandmother's house with his grandmother and his great-aunt Mary and his bachelor uncle. His father had a bicycle-repair shop in the shed behind the house, and his mother worked in Honeker's Department Store.

Jimmy's father was crippled—the result of a polio attack when he was twenty-two years old. He walked bent forward from the hips, using a cane. This didn't show so much when he was working in the shop, because such work often means being bent over anyway. When he walked along the street he did look very strange, but nobody called him names or did an imitation of him. He had once been a notable hockey player and baseball player for the town, and some of the grace and valour of the past still hung around him, putting his present state into perspective, so that it could be seen as a phase (though a final one). He helped this perception along by cracking silly jokes and taking an optimistic tone, denying the pain that showed in his sunken eyes and kept him awake many nights. And, unlike Cece Ferns' father, he didn't change his tune when he came into his own house.

But, of course, it wasn't his own house. His wife had married him after he was crippled, though she had got engaged to him before, and it seemed the natural thing to do to move in with her mother, so that the mother could look after any children who came along while the wife went on working at her job. It seemed the natural thing to the wife's mother as well, to take on another family—just as it seemed natural that her sister Mary should move in with the rest of them when her eyesight failed, and that her son Fred, who was extraordinarily shy, should continue to live at home unless he found some place he liked better. This was a family who accepted burdens of one kind or another with even less fuss than they accepted the weather. In fact, nobody in that house would have spoken of Jimmy's father's condition or Aunt Mary's eyesight as burdens or problems, any more than they would of Fred's shyness. Drawbacks and adversity were not to be noticed, not to be distinguished from their opposites.

There was a traditional belief in the family that Jimmy's grandmother was an excellent cook, and this might have been true at one time, but in recent years there had been a falling off. Economies were practiced beyond what there was any need for now. Jimmy's mother and his uncle made decent wages and his Aunt Mary got a pension and the bicycle shop was fairly busy, but one egg was used instead of three and the meat loaf got an extra cup of oatmeal. There

was an attempt to compensate by overdoing the Worcester-
shire sauce or sprinkling too much nutmeg on the custard.
But nobody complained. Everybody praised. Complaints
were as rare as lightning balls in that house. And everybody
said "Excuse me," even the little girls said "Excuse me,"
when they bumped into each other. Everybody passed and
pleased and thank-you'd at the table as if there were company every day. This was the way they managed, all of them
crammed so tight in the house, with clothes piled on every
hook, coats hung over the banister, and cots set up perma-
nently in the dining-room for Jimmy and his Uncle Fred,
and the buffet hidden under a load of clothing waiting to be
ironed or mended. Nobody pounded on the stairsteps or
shut doors hard or turned the radio up loud or said anything
disagreeable.

Did this explain why Jimmy kept his mouth shut that
Saturday at dinnertime? They all kept their mouths shut,
all three of them. In Cece's case it was easy to understand.
His father would never have stood for Cece's claiming so
important a discovery. He would have called him a liar as a
matter of course. And Cece's mother, judging everything by
the effect it would have on his father, would have understood—correctly—that even his going to the Police Office
with his story would cause disruption at home, so she would
have told him to please just keep quiet. But the two other
boys lived in quite reasonable homes and they could have
spoken. In Jimmy's house there would have been conster-
nation and some disapproval, but soon enough they would
have admitted that it was not Jimmy's fault.

Bud's sisters would have asked if he was crazy. They
might even have twisted things around to imply that it was
just like him, with his unpleasant habits, to come upon a
dead body. His father, however, was a sensible, patient
man, used to listening to many strange rigmaroles in his
job, as a freight agent at the railway station. He would have
made Bud's sisters shut up, and after some serious talk to
make sure Bud was telling the truth and not exaggerating
he would have phoned the Police Office.

It was just that their houses seemed too full. Too much

was going on already. This was true in Cece's house just as much as in the others, because even in his father's absence there was the threat and memory all the time of his haywire presence.

"Did you tell?"
  "Did you?"
  "Me neither."
They walked downtown, not thinking about the way they were going. They turned on to Shipka Street and found themselves going past the stucco bungalow where Mr. and Mrs. Willens lived. They were right in front of it before they recognized it. It had a small bay window on either side of the front door and a top step wide enough for two chairs, not there at present but occupied on summer evenings by Mr. Willens and his wife. There was a flat-roofed addition to one side of the house, with another door opening toward the street and a separate walk leading up to it. A sign beside that door said "D.M. WILLENS, OPTOMETRIST." None of the boys themselves had visited that office, but Jimmy's Aunt Mary went there regularly for her eyedrops, and his grandmother got her glasses there. So did Bud Salter's mother.
The stucco was a muddy pink colour and the doors and window frames were painted brown. The storm windows had not been taken off yet, as they hadn't from most of the houses in town. There was nothing special at all about the house, but the front yard was famous for its flowers. Mrs. Willens was a renowned gardener who didn't grow her flowers in long rows beside the vegetable garden, as Jimmy's grandmother and Bud's mother grew theirs. She had them in round beds and crescent beds and all over, and in circles under the trees. In a couple of weeks daffodils would fill this lawn. But at present the only thing in bloom was a forsythia bush at the corner of the house. It was nearly as high as the eaves and it sprayed yellow into the air the way a fountain shoots water.
The forsythia shook, not with the wind, and out came a stooped brown figure. It was Mrs. Willens in her old

gardening clothes, a lumpy little woman in baggy slacks and a ripped jacket and a peaked cap that might have been her husband's—it slipped down too low and almost hid her eyes. She was carrying a pair of shears.

They slowed right down—it was either that or run. Maybe they thought that she wouldn't notice them, that they could turn themselves into posts. But she had seen them already; that was why she came hastening through.

"I see you're gawking at my forsythia," said Mrs. Willens. "Would you like some to take home?"

What they had been gawking at was not the forsythia but the whole scene—the house looking just as usual, the sign by the office door, the curtains letting light in. Nothing hollow or ominous, nothing that said that Mr. Willens was not inside and that his car was not in the garage behind his office but in Jutland Pond. And Mrs. Willens out working in her yard, where anybody would expect her to be—everybody in town said so—the minute the snow was melted. And calling out in her familiar tobacco-roughened voice, abrupt and challenging but not unfriendly—a voice identifiable half a block away or coming from the back of any store.

"Wait," she said. "Wait, now, I'll get you some."

She began smartly, selectively snapping off the bright-yellow branches, and when she had all she wanted she came toward them behind a screen of flowers.

"Here you are," she said. "Take these home to your mothers. It's always good to see the forsythia, it's the very first thing in the spring." She was dividing the branches among them. "Like all Gaul," she said. "All Gaul is divided into three parts. You must know about that if you take Latin."

"We aren't in high school yet," said Jimmy, whose life at home had readied him, better than the others, for talking to ladies.

"Aren't you?" she said. "Well, you've got all sorts of things to look forward to. Tell your mothers to put them in lukewarm water. Oh, I'm sure they already know that. I've given you branches that aren't all the way out yet, so they should last and last."

They said thank you—Jimmy first and the others picking it up from him. They walked toward downtown with their arms loaded. They had no intention of turning back and taking the flowers home, and they counted on her not having any good idea of where their homes were. Half a block on, they sneaked looks back to see if she was watching.

She wasn't. The big house near the sidewalk blocked the view in any case.

The forsythia gave them something to think about. The embarrassment of carrying it, the problem of getting rid of it. Otherwise, they would have to think about Mr. Willens and Mrs. Willens. How she could be busy in her yard and he could be drowned in his car. Did she know where he was or did she not? It seemed that she couldn't. Did she even know that he was gone? She had acted as if there was nothing wrong, nothing at all, and when they were standing in front of her this had seemed to be the truth. What they knew, what they had seen, seemed actually to be pushed back, to be defeated, by her not knowing it.

Two girls on bicycles came wheeling around the corner. One was Bud's sister Doris. At once these girls began to hoot and yell.

"Oh, look at the flowers," they shouted. "Where's the wedding? Look at the beautiful bridesmaids."

Bud yelled back the worst thing he could think of.

"You got blood all over your arse."

Of course she didn't, but there had been an occasion when this had really been so—she had come home from school with blood on her skirt. Everybody had seen it and it would never be forgotten.

He was sure she would tell on him at home, but she never did. Her shame about that other time was so great that she could not refer to it even to get him in trouble.

They realized then that they had to dump the flowers at once, so they simply threw the branches under a parked car. They brushed a few stray petals off their clothes as they turned on to the square.

Saturdays were still important then; they brought the country people into town. Cars were already parked around the square and on the side streets. Big country boys and girls and smaller children from the town and the country were heading for the movie matinée.

It was necessary to pass Honeker's in the first block. And there, in full view in one of the windows, Jimmy saw his mother. Back at work already, she was putting the hat straight on a female dummy, adjusting the veil, then fiddling with the shoulders of the dress. She was a short woman and she had to stand on tiptoe to do this properly. She had taken off her shoes to walk on the window carpet. You could see the rosy plump cushions of her heels through her stockings, and when she stretched you saw the back of her knee through the slit in her skirt. Above that was a wide but shapely behind and the line of her panties or girdle. Jimmy could hear in his mind the little grunts she would be making; also he could smell the stockings that she sometimes took off as soon as she got home, to save them from runs. Stockings and underwear, even clean female underwear, had a faint, private smell that was both appealing and disgusting.

He hoped two things. That the others hadn't noticed her (they had, but the idea of a mother dressed up every day and out in the public world of town was so strange to them that they couldn't comment, could only dismiss it) and that she would not, please not, turn around and spot him. She was capable, if she did that, of rapping on the glass and mouthing hello. At work she lost the hushed discretion, the studied gentleness, of home. Her obligingness turned from meek to pert. He used to be delighted by this other side of her, this friskiness, just as he was by Honeker's, with its extensive counters of glass and varnished wood, its big mirrors at the top of the staircase, in which he could see himself climbing up to Ladies' Wear, on the second floor.

"Here's my young mischief," his mother would say, and sometimes slip him a dime. He could never stay more than a minute; Mr. or Mrs. Honeker might be watching.

Young mischief.

Words that were once as pleasant to hear as the tinkle of dimes and nickels had now turned slyly shaming.

They were safely past.

In the next block they had to pass the Duke of Cumberland, but Cece had no worries. If his father had not come home at dinnertime, it meant he would be in there for hours yet. But the word "Cumberland" always fell across his mind heavily. From the days when he hadn't even known what it meant, he got a sense of sorrowful plummeting. A weight hitting dark water, far down.

Between the Cumberland and the Town Hall was an unpaved alley, and at the back of the Town Hall was the Police Office. They turned into this alley and soon a lot of new noise reached them, opposing the street noise. It was not from the Cumberland—the noise in there was all muffled up, the beer parlour having only small, high windows like a public toilet. It was coming from the Police Office. The door to that office was open on account of the mild weather, and even out in the alley you could smell the pipe tobacco and cigars. It wasn't just the policemen who sat in there, especially on Saturday afternoons, with the stove going in winter and the fan in summer and the door open to let in the pleasant air on an in-between day like today. Colonel Box would be there—in fact, they could already hear the wheeze he made, the long-drawn-out after-effects of his asthmatic laughter. He was a relative of Jimmy's, but there was a coolness in the family because he did not approve of Jimmy's father's marriage. He spoke to Jimmy, when he recognized him, in a surprised, ironic tone of voice. "If he ever offers you a quarter or anything, you say you don't need it," Jimmy's mother had told him. But Colonel Box had never made such an offer.

Also, Mr. Pollock would be there, who had retired from the drugstore, and Fergus Solley, who was not a half-wit but looked like one, because he had been gassed in the First World War. All day these men and others played cards, smoked, told stories and drank coffee at the town's expense (as Bud's father said). Anybody wanting to make a complaint or a report had to do it within sight of them and probably within earshot.

Run the gauntlet.

They came almost to a stop outside the open door. Nobody had noticed them. Colonel Box said, "I'm not dead yet," repeating the final line of some story. They began to walk past slowly with their heads down, kicking at the gravel. Round the corner of the building they picked up speed. By the entry to the Men's Public Toilet there was a recent streak of lumpy vomit on the wall and a couple of empty bottles on the gravel. They had to walk between the refuse bins and the high watchful windows of the Town Clerk's office, and then they were off the gravel, back on the square.

"I got money," Cece said. This matter-of-fact announcement brought them all relief. Cece jingled change in his pocket. It was the money his mother had given him after he washed up the dishes, when he went into the front bedroom to tell her he was going out. "Help yourself to 50¢ off the dresser," she had said. Sometimes she had money, though he never saw his father give her any. And whenever she said "Help yourself" or gave him a few coins, Cece understood that she was ashamed of their life, ashamed for him and in front of him, and these were the times when he hated the sight of her (though he was glad of the money). Especially if she said that he was a good boy and he was not to think she wasn't grateful for all he did.

They took the street that led down to the harbour. At the side of Paquette's Service Station there was a booth from which Mrs. Paquette sold hotdogs, ice cream, candy and cigarettes. She had refused to sell them cigarettes even when Jimmy said they were for his Uncle Fred. But she didn't hold it against them that they'd tried. She was a fat, pretty woman, a French Canadian.

They bought some licorice whips, black and red. They meant to buy some ice cream later when they weren't so full from dinner. They went over to where there were two old car seats set up by the fence under a tree that gave shade in summer. They shared out the licorice whips.

Captain Tervitt was sitting on the other seat.

Captain Tervitt had been a real captain, for many years, on the lake boats. Now he had a job as a Special Constable. He stopped the cars to let the children cross the street in front of the school and kept them from sledding down the side street in winter. He blew his whistle and held up one big hand, which looked like a clown's hand, in a white glove. He was still tall and straight and broad-shouldered, though old and white-haired. Cars would do what he said, and children, too.

At night he went around checking the doors of all the stores to see that they were locked and to make sure that there was nobody inside committing a burglary. During the day he often slept in public. When the weather was bad he slept in the library and when it was good he chose some seat out-of-doors. He didn't spend much time in the Police Office, probably because he was too deaf to follow the conversation without his hearing aid in, and like many deaf people he hated his hearing aid. And he was used to being solitary, surely, staring out over the bow of the lake boats.

His eyes were closed and his head tilted back so that he could get the sun in his face. When they went over to talk to him (and the decision to do this was made without any consultation, beyond one resigned and dubious look) they had to wake him from his doze. His face took a moment to register—where and when and who. Then he took a large old-fashioned watch out of his pocket, as if he counted on children always wanting to be told the time. But they went on talking to him, with their expressions agitated and slightly shamed. They were saying, "Mr. Willens is out in Jutland Pond," and "We seen the car," and "Drowned." He had to hold up his hand and make shushing motions while the other hand went rooting around in his pants pocket and came up with his hearing aid. He nodded his head seriously, encouragingly, as if to say, "Patience, patience," while he got the device settled in his ear. Then both hands up—be still, be still—while he was testing. Finally another nod, of a brisker sort, and in a stern voice— but making a joke to some extent of his sternness—he said, "Proceed."

Cece, who was the quietest of the three—as Jimmy was the politest and Bud the mouthiest—was the one who turned everything around.

"Your fly's undone," he said.

Then they all whooped and ran away. The jolt of freedom, the joy of outrage, the uttermost trespass.

Their elation did not vanish right away. But it was not something that could be shared or spoken about: they had to pull apart.

Cece went home to work on his hideaway. The cardboard floor, which had been frozen through the winter, was sodden now and needed to be replaced. Jimmy climbed into the loft of the garage, where he had recently discovered a box of old Doc Savage magazines that had once belonged to his Uncle Fred. Bud went home and found nobody there but his mother, who was waxing the dining-room floor. He looked at comic books for an hour or so and then he told her. He believed that his mother had no experience or authority outside their house and that she would not make up her mind about what to do until she had phoned his father. To his surprise, she immediately phoned the police. Then she phoned his father. And somebody went to round up Cece and Jimmy.

A police car drove in to Jutland from the township road, and all was confirmed. A policeman and the Anglican minister went to see Mrs. Willens.

"I didn't want to bother you," Mrs. Willens was reported to have said. "I was going to give him till dark."

She told them that Mr. Willens had driven out to the country yesterday afternoon to take some drops to an old blind man. Sometimes he got held up, she said. He visited people, or the car got stuck.

Was he downhearted or anything like that? the policeman asked her.

"Oh, surely not," the minister said. "He was the bulwark of the choir."

"The word was not in his vocabulary," said Mrs. Willens.

Something was made of the boys' sitting down and

146

eating their dinners and never saying a word. And then buying a bunch of licorice whips. A new nickname—Deadman—was found and settled on each of them. Jimmy and Bud bore it till they left town, and Cece—who married young and went to work in the elevator—saw it passed on to his two sons. By that time nobody thought of what it referred to.

The insult to Captain Tervitt remained a secret.

Each of them expected some reminder, some lofty look of injury or judgment, the next time they had to pass under his uplifted arm, crossing the street to the school. But he held up his gloved hand, his noble and clownish white hand, with his usual benevolent composure. He gave consent.

Proceed.

II. HEART FAILURE

"Glomerulonephritis," Enid wrote in her notebook. It was the first case that she had ever seen. The fact was that Mrs. Quinn's kidneys were failing, and nothing could be done about it. Her kidneys were drying up and turning into hard and useless granular lumps. Her urine at present was scanty and had a smoky look, and the smell that came out on her breath and through her skin was acrid and ominous. And there was another, fainter smell, like rotted fruit, that seemed to Enid related to the pale lavender-brown stains appearing on her body. Her legs twitched in spasms of sudden pain and her skin was subject to a violent itching, so that Enid had to rub her with ice. She wrapped the ice in towels and pressed the packs to the spots in torment.

"How do you contract that kind of a disease anyhow?" said Mrs. Quinn's sister-in-law. Her name was Mrs. Green. Olive Green. (It had never occurred to her how that would sound, she said, until she got married and all of a sudden everybody was laughing at it.) She lived on a farm a few miles away, out on the highway, and every few days she came and took the sheets and towels and nightdresses away to wash. She did the children's washing as well, brought everything back freshly ironed and folded. She even ironed the ribbons on the nightdresses. Enid was grateful to her—she had been on jobs where she had to do the laundry herself, or, worse still, load it onto her mother, who would pay to have it done in town. Not wanting to offend but seeing which way the questions were tending, she said, "It's hard to tell."

"Because you hear one thing and another," Mrs. Green said. "You hear that sometimes a woman might take some pills. They get these pills to take for when their period is late and if they take them just like the doctor says and for a good purpose that's fine, but if they take too many and for a bad purpose their kidneys are wrecked. Am I right?"

"I've never come in contact with a case like that," Enid said.

Mrs. Green was a tall, stout woman. Like her brother Rupert, who was Mrs. Quinn's husband, she had a round, snub-nosed, agreeably wrinkled face—the kind that Enid's mother called "potato Irish." But behind Rupert's good-humoured expression there was wariness and withholding. And behind Mrs. Green's there was yearning. Enid did not know for what. To the simplest conversation Mrs. Green brought a huge demand. Maybe it was just a yearning for news. News of something momentous. An event.

Of course, an event was coming, something momentous at least in this family. Mrs. Quinn was going to die, at the age of twenty-seven. (That was the age she gave herself—Enid would have put some years on it, but once an illness had progressed this far age was hard to guess.) When her kidneys stopped working altogether, her heart would give out and she would die. The doctor had said to Enid, "This'll take you into the summer, but the chances are you'll get some kind of a holiday before the hot weather's over."

"Rupert met her when he went up north," Mrs. Green said. "He went off by himself, he worked in the bush up there. She had some kind of a job in a hotel. I'm not sure what. Chambermaid job. She wasn't raised up there, though—she says she was raised in an orphanage in

Montreal. She can't help that. You'd expect her to speak French, but if she does she don't let on."

Enid said, "An interesting life."

"You can say that again."

"An interesting life," said Enid. Sometimes she couldn't help it—she tried a joke where it had hardly a hope of working. She raised her eyebrows encouragingly, and Mrs. Green did smile.

But was she hurt? That was just the way Rupert would smile, in high school, warding off some possible mockery.

"He never had any kind of a girlfriend before that," said Mrs. Green.

Enid had been in the same class as Rupert, though she did not mention that to Mrs. Green. She felt some embarrassment now because he was one of the boys—in fact, the main one—that she and her girlfriends had teased and tormented. "Picked on," as they used to say. They had picked on Rupert, following him up the street calling out, "Hello, Ru-pert. Hello, Ru-pert," putting him into a state of agony, watching his neck go red. "Rupert's got scarlet fever," they would say. "Rupert, you should be quarantined." And they would pretend that one of them—Enid, Joan McAuliffe, Marian Denny—had a case on him. "She wants to speak to you, Rupert. Why don't you ever ask her out? You could phone her up at least. She's dying to talk to you."

They did not really expect him to respond to these pleading overtures. But what joy if he had. He would have been rejected in short order and the story broadcast all over the school. Why? Why did they treat him this way, long to humiliate him? Simply because they could.

Impossible that he would have forgotten. But he treated Enid as if she were a new acquaintance, his wife's nurse, come into his house from anywhere at all. And Enid took her cue from him.

Things had been unusually well arranged here, to spare her extra work. Rupert slept at Mrs. Green's house, and ate his meals there. The two little girls could have been there as well, but it would have meant putting them into another school—there was nearly a month to go before school was out for the summer.

Rupert came into the house in the evenings and spoke to his children.

"Are you being good girls?" he said.

"Show Daddy what you made with your blocks," said Enid. "Show Daddy your pictures in the colouring book."

The blocks, the crayons, the colouring books were all provided by Enid. She had phoned her mother and asked her to see what things she could find in the old trunks. Her mother had done that, and brought along as well an old book of cutout dolls which she had collected from someone—Princesses Elizabeth and Margaret Rose and their many outfits. Enid hadn't been able to get the little girls to say thank you until she put all these things on a high shelf and announced that they would stay there till thank you was said. Lois and Sylvie were seven and six years old, and as wild as little barn cats.

Rupert didn't ask where the playthings came from. He told his daughters to be good girls and asked Enid if there was anything she needed from town. Once she told him that she had replaced the lightbulb in the cellarway and that he could get her some spare bulbs.

"I could have done that," he said.

"I don't have any trouble with lightbulbs," said Enid. "Or fuses or knocking in nails. My mother and I have done without a man around the house for a long time now." She meant to tease a little, to be friendly, but it didn't work.

Finally Rupert would ask about his wife, and Enid would say that her blood pressure was down slightly, or that she had eaten and kept down part of an omelet for supper, or that the ice packs seemed to ease her itchy skin and she was sleeping better. And Rupert would say that if she was sleeping he'd better not go in.

Enid said, "Nonsense." To see her husband would do a woman more good than to have a little doze. She took the children up to bed then, to give man and wife a time of privacy. But Rupert never stayed more than a few minutes. And when Enid came back downstairs and went into the front room—now the sickroom—to ready the patient for the night, Mrs. Quinn would be lying back against the pillows, looking agitated but not dissatisfied.

"Doesn't hang around here very long, does he?" Mrs. Quinn would say. "Makes me laugh. Ha-ha-ha, how-are-you? Ha-ha-ha, off-we-go. Why don't we take her out and throw her on the manure pile? Why don't we just dump her out like a dead cat? That's what he's thinking. Isn't he?"

"I doubt it," said Enid, bringing the basin and towels, the rubbing alcohol and the baby powder.

"I doubt it," said Mrs. Quinn quite viciously, but she submitted readily enough to having her nightgown removed, her hair smoothed back from her face, a towel slid under her hips. Enid was used to people making a fuss about being naked, even when they were very old or very ill. Sometimes she would have to tease them or badger them into common sense. "Do you think I haven't seen any bottom parts before?" she would say. "Bottom parts, top parts, it's pretty boring after a while. You know, there's just the two ways we're made." But Mrs. Quinn was without shame, opening her legs and raising herself a bit to make the job easier. She was a little bird-boned woman, queerly shaped now, with her swollen abdomen and limbs and her breasts shrunk to tiny pouches with dried-currant nipples.

"Swole up like some kind of pig," Mrs. Quinn said. "Except for my tits, and they always were kind of useless. I never had no big udders on me, like you. Don't you get sick of the sight of me? Won't you be glad when I'm dead?"

"If I felt like that I wouldn't be here," said Enid.

"Good riddance to bad rubbish," said Mrs. Quinn. "That's what you'll all say. Good riddance to bad rubbish. I'm no use to him anymore, am I? I'm no use to any man. He goes out of here every night and he goes to pick up women, doesn't he?"

"As far as I know, he goes to his sister's house."

"As far as you know. But you don't know much."

Enid thought she knew what this meant, this spite and venom, the energy saved for ranting. Mrs. Quinn was flailing about for an enemy. Sick people grew to resent well people, and sometimes that was true of husbands and wives, or even of mothers and their children. Both husband and children in Mrs. Quinn's case. On a Saturday morning, Enid called Lois and Sylvie from their games under the porch, to come and see their mother looking pretty. Mrs. Quinn had just had her morning wash, and was in a clean nightgown, with her fine, sparse, fair hair brushed and held back by a blue ribbon. (Enid took a supply of these ribbons with her when she went to nurse a female patient—also a bottle of cologne and a cake of scented soap.) She did look pretty—or you could see at least that she had once been pretty, with her wide forehead and cheekbones (they almost punched the skin now, like china doorknobs) and her large greenish eyes and childish translucent teeth and small stubborn chin.

The children came into the room obediently if unenthusiastically.

Mrs. Quinn said, "Keep them off of my bed, they're filthy."

"They just want to see you," said Enid.

"Well, now they've seen me," said Mrs. Quinn. "Now they can go."

This behaviour didn't seem to surprise or disappoint the children. They looked at Enid, and Enid said, "All right, now, your mother better have a rest," and they ran out and slammed the kitchen door.

"Can't you get them to quit doing that?" Mrs. Quinn said. "Every time they do it, it's like a brick hits me in my chest."

You would think these two daughters of hers were a pair of rowdy orphans, wished on her for an indefinite visit. But that was the way some people were, before they settled down to their dying and sometimes even up to the event itself. People of a gentler nature—it would seem—than Mrs. Quinn might say that they knew how much their brothers, sisters, husbands, wives and children had always hated them, how much of a disappointment they had been to others and others had been to them, and how glad they knew everybody would be to see them gone. They might say this at the end of peaceful, useful lives in the midst of loving families, where there was no explanation at all for such fits. And usually the fits passed. But often, too, in the last weeks or even days of life there was mulling over of old feuds and slights or whimpering about some unjust punishment suffered 70 years earlier. Once a woman had asked Enid to bring her a willow platter from the cupboard and Enid had thought that she wanted the comfort of looking at this one pretty possession for the last time. But it turned out that she wanted to use her last, surprising strength to smash it against the bedpost.

"Now I know my sister's never going to get her hands on that," she said.

And often people remarked that their visitors were only coming to gloat and that the doctor was responsible for their sufferings. They detested the sight of Enid herself, for her sleepless strength and patient hands and the way the juices of life were so admirably balanced and flowing in her. Enid was used to that, and she was able to understand the trouble they were in, the trouble of dying and also the trouble of their lives that sometimes overshadowed that.

But with Mrs. Quinn she was at a loss.

It was not just that she couldn't supply comfort here. It was that she couldn't want to. She could not conquer her dislike of this doomed, miserable young woman. She disliked this body that she had to wash and powder and placate with ice and alcohol rubs. She understood now what people meant when they said that they hated sickness and sick bodies; she understood the women who had said to her, I don't know how you do it, I could never be a nurse, that's the one thing I could never be. She disliked this particular body, all the particular signs of its disease. The smell of it and the discoloration, the malignant-looking little nipples and the pathetic ferretlike teeth. She saw all this as the sign of a willed corruption. She was as bad as Mrs. Green, sniffing out rampant impurity. In spite of being a nurse who knew better, and in spite of it being her job—and surely her nature—to be compassionate. She didn't know why this was happening. Mrs. Quinn reminded her somewhat of girls she had known in high school—cheaply dressed, sickly-looking girls with dreary futures, who still displayed a hard-faced satisfaction with themselves. They lasted only a year or two—they got pregnant, most of them got married. Enid had nursed some of them in later years, in home childbirth, and found their confidence exhausted and their bold streak turned into meekness, or even piety. She was sorry for them, even when she remembered how determined they had been to get what they had got.

Mrs. Quinn was a harder case. Mrs. Quinn might crack and crack, but there would be nothing but sullen mischief, nothing but rot inside her.

Worse even than the fact that Enid should feel this revulsion was the fact that Mrs. Quinn knew it. No patience or gentleness or cheerfulness that Enid could summon would keep Mrs. Quinn from knowing. And Mrs. Quinn made knowing it her triumph.

Good riddance to bad rubbish.

When Enid was twenty years old, and had almost finished her nurse's training, her father was dying in the Walley hospital. That was when he said to her, "I don't know as I care for this career of yours. I don't want you working in a place like this."

Enid bent over him and asked what sort of place he thought he was in. "It's only the Walley hospital," she said.

"I know that," said her father, sounding as calm and reasonable as he had always done (he was an insurance and real-estate agent). "I know what I'm talking about. Promise me you won't."

"Promise you what?" said Enid.

"You won't do this kind of work," her father said. She could not get any further explanation out of him. He tightened up his mouth as if her questioning disgusted him. All he would say was, "Promise."

"What is all this about?" Enid asked her mother, and her mother said, "Oh, go ahead. Go ahead and promise him. What difference is it going to make?"

Enid thought this a shocking thing to say, but made no

comment. It was consistent with her mother's way of looking at a lot of things.

"I'm not going to promise anything I don't understand," she said. "I'm probably not going to promise anything anyway. But if you know what he's talking about you ought to tell me."

"It's just this idea he's got now," her mother said. "He's got an idea that nursing makes a woman coarse."

Enid said, "Coarse."

Her mother said that the part of nursing her father objected to was the familiarity nurses had with men's bodies. Her father thought—he had decided—that such familiarity would change a girl, and furthermore that it would change the way men thought about that girl. It would spoil her good chances and give her a lot of other chances that were not so good. Some men would lose interest and others would become interested in the wrong way.

"I suppose it's all mixed up with wanting you to get married," he mother said.

"Too bad if it is," said Enid.

But she ended up promising. And her mother said, "Well, I hope that makes you happy." Not "makes him happy." Makes *you*. It seemed that her mother had known before Enid did just how tempting this promise would be. The deathbed promise, the self-denial, the wholesale sacrifice. And the more absurd the better. This was what she had given in to. And not for love of her father, either (her mother implied), but for the thrill of it. Sheer noble perversity.

"If he'd asked you to give up something you didn't care one way or the other about, you'd probably have told him nothing doing," her mother said. "If for instance he'd asked you to give up wearing lipstick. You'd still be wearing it."

Enid listened to this with a patient expression.

"Did you pray about it?" said her mother sharply.

Enid said yes.

She withdrew from nursing school; she stayed at home and kept busy. There was enough money that she did not have to work. In fact, her mother had not wanted Enid to go into nursing in the first place, claiming that it was something poor girls did, it was a way out for girls whose parents couldn't keep them or send them to college. Enid did not remind her of this inconsistency. She painted a fence, she tied up the rosebushes for winter. She learned to bake and she learned to play bridge, taking her father's place in the weekly games her mother played with Mr. and Mrs. Willens from next door. In no time at all she became—as Mr. Willens said—a scandalously good player. He took to turning up with chocolates or a pink rose for her, to make up for his own inadequacies as a partner.

She went skating in the winter evenings. She played badminton.

She had never lacked friends, and she didn't now. Most of the people who had been in the last year of high school with her were finishing college now, or were already working at a distance, as teachers or nurses or chartered accountants. But she made friends with others who had dropped out before senior year to work in banks or stores or offices, to become plumbers or milliners. The girls in this group were dropping like flies, as they said of each other—they were dropping into matrimony. Enid was an organizer of bridal showers and a help at trousseau teas. In a couple of years would come the christenings, where she could expect to be a favourite godmother. Children not related to her would grow up calling her Aunt. And she was already a sort of honorary daughter to women of her mother's age and older, the only young woman who had time for the Book Club and the Horticultural Society. So, quickly and easily, still in her youth, she was slipping into this essential, central, yet isolated role.

But in fact it had been her role all along. In high school she was always the class secretary or class social convener. She was well liked and high-spirited and well dressed and good-looking, but she was slightly set apart. She had friends who were boys but never a boyfriend. She did not seem to have made a choice this way, but she was not worried about it, either. She had been preoccupied with her ambition—to be a missionary, at one embarrassing stage, and then to be a nurse. She had never thought of nursing as just something to do until she got married. Her hope was to be good, and do good, and not necessarily in the orderly, customary, wifely way.

At New Year's she went to the dance in the Town Hall. The man who danced with her most often, and escorted her home, and pressed her hand goodnight, was the manager of the creamery—a man in his forties, never married, an excellent dancer, an avuncular friend to girls unlikely to find partners. No woman ever took him seriously.

"Maybe you should take a business course," her mother said. "Or why shouldn't you go to college?"

Where the men might be more appreciative, she was surely thinking.

"I'm too old," said Enid.

Her mother laughed. "That only shows how young you are," she said. She seemed relieved to discover that her daughter had a touch of folly natural to her age—that she could think twenty-one was at a vast distance from eighteen.

"I'm not going to troop in with kids out of high school," Enid said. "I mean it. What do you want to get rid of me for anyway? I'm fine here." This sulkiness or sharpness also seemed to please and reassure her mother. But after a moment she sighed, and said, "You'll be surprised how fast the years go by."

That August there were a lot of cases of measles and a few of polio at the same time. The doctor who had looked after Enid's father, and had observed her competence around the hospital, asked her if she would be willing to help out for a while, nursing people at home. She said that she would think about it.

"You mean pray?" her mother said, and Enid's face took on a stubborn, secretive expression that in another girl's case might have had to do with meeting her boyfriend.

"That promise," she said to her mother the next day. "That was about working in a hospital, wasn't it?"

Her mother said that she had understood it that way, yes.

"And with graduating and being a registered nurse?"

Yes, yes.

So if there were people who needed nursing at home, who couldn't afford to go to the hospital or did not want to go, and if Enid went into their houses to nurse them, not as a registered nurse but as what they called a practical nurse, she would hardly be breaking her promise, would she? And since most of those needing her care would be children or women having babies, or old people dying, there would not be much danger of the coarsening effect, would there?

"If the only men you get to see are men who are never going to get out of bed again, you have a point," said her mother.

But she could not keep from adding that what all this meant was that Enid had decided to give up the possibility of a decent job in a hospital in order to do miserable back-breaking work in miserable primitive houses for next to no money. Enid would find herself pumping water from contaminated wells and breaking ice in winter washbasins and battling flies in summer and using an outdoor toilet. Scrub-boards and coal-oil lamps instead of washing machines and electricity. Trying to look after sick people in those conditions and cope with housework and poor weaselly children as well.

"But if that is your object in life," she said, "I can see that the worse I make it sound the more determined you get to do it. The only thing is, I'm going to ask for a couple of promises myself. Promise me you'll boil the water you drink. And you won't marry a farmer."

Enid said, "Of all the crazy ideas."

That was sixteen years ago. During the first of those years people got poorer and poorer. There were more and more of them who could not afford to go to the hospital, and the houses where Enid worked had often deteriorated almost to the state that her mother had described. Sheets and diapers had to be washed by hand in houses where the washing machine had broken down and could not be repaired, or the electricity had been turned off, or where there had never been any electricity in the first place. Enid did not work without pay, because that would not have been fair to the other women who did the same kind of nursing, and who did not have the same options as she did. But she gave most of the money back, in the form of children's shoes and winter coats and trips to the dentist and Christmas toys.

Her mother went around canvassing her friends for old baby cots, and highchairs and blankets, and worn-out sheets, which she herself ripped up and hemmed to make diapers. Everybody said how proud she must be of Enid, and she said yes, she surely was.

"But sometimes it's a devil of a lot of work," she said. "This being the mother of a saint."

Then came the war, and the great shortage of doctors and nurses, and Enid was more welcome than ever. As she was for a while after the war, with so many babies being born. It was only now, with the hospitals being enlarged and many farms getting prosperous, that it looked as if her responsibilities might dwindle away to the care of those who had bizarre and hopeless afflictions, or were so irredeemably cranky that hospitals had thrown them out.

This summer there was a great downpour of rain every few days, and then the sun came out very hot, glittering off the drenched leaves and grass. Early mornings were full of mist—they were so close, here, to the river—and even when the mist cleared off you could not see very far in any direction, because of the overflow and density of summer. The heavy trees, the bushes all bound up with wild grapevines and Virginia creeper, the crops of corn and barley and wheat and hay. Everything was ahead of itself, as people said. The hay was ready to cut in June, and Rupert had to rush to get it into the barn before a rain spoiled it.

He came into the house later and later in the evenings, having worked as long as the light lasted. One night when he came the house was in darkness, except for a candle burning on the kitchen table.

Enid hurried to unhook the screendoor.

"Power out?" said Rupert.

Enid said, "Sh-h-h." She whispered to him that she was letting the children sleep downstairs, because the upstairs rooms were so hot. She had pushed the chairs together and made beds on them with quilts and pillows. And of course she had had to turn the lights out so that they could get to sleep. She had found a candle in one of the drawers, and that was all she needed, to see to write by, in her notebook.

"They'll always remember sleeping here," she said. "You always remember the times when you were a child and you slept somewhere different."

He set down a box that contained a ceiling fan for the sickroom. He had been in to Walley to buy it. He had also bought a newspaper, which he handed to Enid.

"Thought you might like to know what's going on in the world," he said.

She spread the paper out beside her notebook, on the table. There was a picture of a couple of dogs playing in a fountain.

"It says there's a heatwave," she said. "Isn't it nice to find out about it?"

Rupert was carefully lifting the fan out of its box.

"That'll be wonderful," she said. "It's cooled off in there now, but it'll be such a comfort to her tomorrow."

"I'll be over early to put it up," he said. Then he asked how his wife had been that day.

Enid said that the pains in her legs had been easing off, and the new pills the doctor had her on seemed to be letting her get some rest.

"The only thing is, she goes to sleep so soon," she said. "It makes it hard for you to get a visit."

"Better she gets the rest," Rupert said.

This whispered conversation reminded Enid of conversations in high school, when they were both in their senior year and that earlier teasing, or cruel flirtation, or whatever it was, had long been abandoned. All that last year Rupert had sat in the seat behind hers, and they had often spoken to each other briefly, always to some immediate purpose.

Have you got an ink eraser? How do you spell "incriminate?" Where is the Tyrrhenian Sea? Usually it was Enid, half turning in her seat and able only to sense, not see, how close Rupert was, who started these conversations. She did want to borrow an eraser, she was in need of information, but also she wanted to be sociable. And she wanted to make amends—she felt ashamed of the way she and her friends had treated him. It would do no good to apologize—that would just embarrass him all over again. He was only at ease when he sat behind her, and knew that she could not look him in the face. If they met on the street he would look away until the last minute, then mutter the faintest greeting while she sang out "Hello, Rupert," and heard an echo of the old tormenting tones she wanted to banish.

But when he actually laid a finger on her shoulder, tapping for attention, when he bent forward, almost touching or maybe really touching—she could not tell for sure—her dark thick hair that was wild even in a bob, then she felt forgiven. In a way, she felt honored. Restored to seriousness and to respect.

Where, where exactly, is the Tyrrhenian Sea?

She wondered if he remembered anything at all of that now.

She separated the back and front parts of the paper. Margaret Truman was visiting England, and had curtsied to the Royal Family. The King's doctors were trying to cure his Buerger's disease with Vitamin E.

She offered the front part to Rupert. "I'm going to look at the crossword," she said. "I like to do the crossword—it relaxes me at the end of the day."

Rupert sat down and began to read the paper, and she asked him if he would like a cup of tea. Of course he said not to bother, and she went ahead and made it anyway, understanding that this reply might as well be yes in country speech.

"It's a South American theme," she said, looking at the crossword. "Latin-American theme. First across is a musical *garment*. A musical garment? Garment. A lot of letters. Oh. Oh. I'm lucky tonight. Cape Horn!

"You see how silly they are, these things," she said, and rose and poured the tea.

If he did remember, did he hold anything against her? Maybe her blithe friendliness in their senior year had been as unwelcome, as superior-seeming to him, as that early taunting?

When she first saw him in this house, she thought that he had not changed much. He had been a tall, solid, round-faced boy, and he was a tall, heavy, round-faced man. He had worn his hair cut so short, always, that it didn't make much difference that there was less of it now and that it had turned from light brown to grey brown. A permanent sunburn had taken the place of his blushes. And whatever troubled him and showed in his face might have been just the same old trouble—the problem of occupying space in the world and having a name that people could call you by, being somebody they thought they could know.

She thought of them sitting in the senior class. A small class, by that time—in five years the unstudious, the carefree and the indifferent had been weeded out, leaving these overgrown, grave and docile children learning trigonometry, learning Latin. What kind of life did they think they were preparing for? What kind of people did they think they were going to be?

She could see the dark-green, softened cover of a book called "History of the Renaissance and Reformation." It was secondhand, or tenthhand—nobody ever bought a new textbook. Inside were written all the names of the previous owners, some of whom were middle-aged housewives or merchants around the town. You could not imagine them learning these things, or underlining "Edict of Nantes" with red ink and writing "N.B." in the margin.

Edict of Nantes. The very uselessness, the exotic nature of the things in those books and in those students' heads, in her own head then and Rupert's, made Enid feel a tenderness and wonder. It wasn't that they had meant to be something that they hadn't become. Nothing like that. Rupert couldn't have imagined anything but farming this farm. It was a good farm, and he was an only son. And she herself had ended up doing exactly what she must have wanted to do. You couldn't say that they had chosen the wrong lives or chosen against their will or not understood their choices. Just that they had not understood how time would pass and leave them not more but maybe a little less than what they used to be.

"Bread of the Amazon," she said. "Bread of the Amazon?"

Rupert said, "Manioc?"

Enid counted. "Seven letters," she said. "Seven."

He said, "Cassava?"

"Cassava? That's a double 's'? Cassava."

Mrs. Quinn became more capricious daily about her food. Sometimes she said she wanted toast, or bananas with milk on them. One day she said peanut-butter cookies. Enid prepared all these things—the children could eat them anyway—and when they were ready Mrs. Quinn could not stand the look or the smell of them. Even jello had a smell she could not stand.

Some days she hated all noise; she would not even have the fan going. Other days she wanted the radio on, she wanted the station that played requests for birthdays and anniversaries and called people up to ask them questions. If you got the answer right you won a trip to Niagara Falls, a tankful of gas, or a load of groceries or tickets to a movie.

"It's all fixed," Mrs. Quinn said. "They just pretend to call somebody up—they're in the next room and already got the answer told to them. I used to know somebody that worked for a radio, that's the truth."

On these days her pulse was rapid. She talked very fast in a light, breathless voice. "What kind of car is that your mother's got?" she said.

"It's a maroon-coloured car," said Enid.

"What *make*?" said Mrs. Quinn.

Enid said she did not know, which was the truth. She had known, but she had forgotten.

"Was it new when she got it?"

"Yes," said Enid. "Yes. But that was three or four years ago."

"She lives in that big rock house next door to Willenses'?"
Yes, said Enid.

"How many rooms it got? Sixteen?"

"Too many."

"Did you go to Mr. Willens' funeral when he got drownded?"

Enid said no. "I'm not much for funerals."

"I was supposed to go. I wasn't awfully sick then, I was going with Herveys up the highway, they said I could get a ride with them and then her mother and her sister wanted to go and there wasn't enough room in back. Then Clive and Olive went and I could've scrunched up in their front seat but they never thought to ask me. Do you think he drownded himself?"

Enid thought of Mr. Willens handing her a rose. His jokey gallantry that made the nerves of her teeth ache, as from too much sugar.

"I don't know. I wouldn't think so."

"Did him and Mrs. Willens get along all right?"

"As far as I know, they got along beautifully."

"Oh, is that so?" said Mrs. Quinn, trying to imitate Enid's reserved tone. "Bee-you-tif-ley."

Enid slept on the couch in Mrs. Quinn's room. Mrs. Quinn's devastating itch had almost disappeared, as had her need to urinate. She slept through most of the night, though she would have spells of harsh and angry breathing. What woke Enid up and kept her awake was a trouble of her own. She had begun to have ugly dreams. These were unlike any dreams she had ever had before. She used to think that a bad dream was one of finding herself in an unfamiliar house where the rooms kept changing and there was always more work to do than she could handle, work undone that she thought she had done, innumerable distractions. And then, of course, she had what she thought of as romantic dreams, in which some man would have his arm around her or even be embracing her. It might be a stranger or a man she knew—sometimes a man whom it was quite a joke to think of in that way. These dreams made her thoughtful or a little sad but relieved in some way to know that such feelings were possible for her. They could be embarrassing, but were nothing, nothing at all compared with the dreams that she was having now. In the dreams that came to her now she would be copulating or trying to copulate (sometimes she was prevented by intruders or shifts of circumstances) with utterly forbidden and unthinkable partners. With fat squirmy babies or patients in bandages or her own mother. She would be slick with lust, hollow and groaning with it, and she would set to work with roughness and an attitude of evil pragmatism. "Yes, this will have to do," she would say to herself. "This will do if nothing better comes along." And this coldness of heart, this matter-of-fact depravity, simply drove her lust along. She woke up unrepentant, sweaty and exhausted, and lay like a carcase until her own self, her shame and disbelief, came pouring back into her. The sweat went cold on her skin. She lay there shivering in the warm night, with disgust and humiliation. She did not dare go back to sleep. She got used to the dark and the long rectangles of the net-curtained windows filled with a faint light. And the sick woman's breath grating and scolding and then almost disappearing.

If she were a Catholic, she thought, was this the sort of thing that could come out at confession? It didn't seem like the sort of thing she could even bring out in a private prayer. She didn't pray much anymore, except formally, and to bring the experiences she had just been through to the attention of God seemed absolutely useless, disrespectful. He would be insulted. She was insulted, by her own mind. Her religion was hopeful and sensible and there was no room in it for any sort of rubbishy drama, such as the invasion of the Devil into her sleep. The filth in her mind was in her, and there was no point in dramatizing it and making it seem important. Surely not. It was nothing, just the mind's garbage.

In the little meadow between the house and the riverbank there were cows. She could hear them munching and jostling, feeding at night. She thought of their large gentle shapes in there with the money musk and chicory, the flowering grasses, and she thought, They have a lovely life, cows.

It ends, of course, in the slaughterhouse. The end is disaster.

For everybody, though, the same thing. Evil grabs us when we are sleeping; pain and disintegration lie in wait. Animal horrors, all worse than you can imagine beforehand. The comforts of bed and the cows' breath, the pattern of the stars at night—all that can get turned on its head in an instant. And here she was, here was Enid, working her life away pretending it wasn't so. Trying to ease people. Trying to be good. An angel of mercy, as her mother had said, with less and less irony as time went on. Patients and doctors, too, had said it.

And all the time how many thought that she was a fool? The people she spent her labours on might secretly despise her. Thinking they'd never do the same in her place. Never be fool enough. No.

Miserable offenders, came into her head. *Miserable offenders. Restore them that are penitent.*

So she got up and went to work; as far as she was concerned, that was the best way to be penitent. She worked very quietly but steadily through the night, washing the cloudy glasses and sticky plates that were in the cupboards and establishing order where there was none before. None. Teacups had sat between the ketchup and the mustard and toilet paper on top of a pail of honey. There was no waxed paper or even newspaper laid out on the shelves. Brown sugar in the bag was as hard as rock. It was understandable that things should have gone downhill in the last few months, but it looked as if there had been no care, no organization here, ever. All the net curtains were grey with smoke and the windowpanes were greasy. The last bit of jam had been left to grow fuzz in the jar, and vile-smelling water that had held some ancient bouquet had never been dumped out of its jug. But there was a good house still, that scrubbing and painting could restore. But what could you do about the ugly brown paint that had been recently and sloppily applied to the front-room floor?

When she had a moment later in the day she pulled the weeds out of Rupert's mother's flowerbeds, dug up the burdocks and twitch grass that were smothering the valiant perennials.

She taught the children to hold their spoons properly and to say grace.

Thank you for the world so sweet,

Thank you for the food we eat....

She taught them to brush their teeth and after that to say their prayers.

"God bless Mama and Daddy and Enid and Aunt Olive and Uncle Clive and Princess Elizabeth and Margaret Rose." After that each added the name of the other. They had been doing it for quite a while when Sylvie said, "What does it mean?"

Enid said, "What does what mean?"

"What does it mean 'God bless'?"

Enid made eggnogs, not flavouring them even with vanilla, and fed them to Mrs. Quinn from a spoon. She fed her a little of the rich liquid at a time, and Mrs. Quinn was able to hold down what was given to her in small amounts. If she could not do that, Enid spooned out flat, lukewarm ginger ale.

The sunlight, or any light, was as hateful as noise to Mrs. Quinn by now. Enid had to hang thick quilts over the windows, even when the blinds were pulled down. With the fan shut off, as Mrs. Quinn demanded, the room became very hot, and sweat dripped from Enid's forehead as she bent over the bed attending to the patient. Mrs. Quinn went into fits of shivering; she could never be warm enough.

"This is dragging out," the doctor said. "It must be those milkshakes you're giving her, keeping her going."

"Eggnogs," said Enid, as if it mattered.

Mrs. Quinn was often now too tired or weak to talk. Sometimes she lay in a stupor, with her breathing so faint and her pulse so lost and wandering that a person less experienced than Enid would have taken her for dead. But at other times she rallied, wanted the radio on, then wanted it off. She knew perfectly well who she was still, and who Enid was, and she sometimes seemed to be watching Enid with a speculative or inquiring look in her eyes. The colour was long gone from her face and even from her lips, but her eyes looked greener than they had in the past—a milky, cloudy green. Enid tried to answer the look that was bent on her.

"Would you like me to get a priest to talk to you?"

Mrs. Quinn looked as if she wanted to spit.

"Do I look like a Mick?" she said.

"A minister?" said Enid. She knew this was the right thing to ask, but the spirit in which she asked it was not right—it was cold and faintly malicious.

No. This was not what Mrs. Quinn wanted. She grunted with displeasure. There was some energy in her still, and Enid had the feeling that she was building it up for a purpose. "Do you want to talk to your children?" she said, making herself speak compassionately and encouragingly. "Is that what you want?"

No.

"Your husband? Your husband will be here in a little while."

Enid didn't know that for sure. Rupert arrived late some nights, after Mrs. Quinn had taken the final pills and gone to sleep. Then he sat with Enid. He always brought her the newspaper. He asked what she wrote in her notebooks—he noticed that there were two—and she told him. One for the doctor, with a record of blood pressure and pulse and temperature, a record of what was eaten, vomited, excreted, medicines taken, some general summing up of the patient's condition. In the other notebook, for herself, she wrote many of the same things, though perhaps not so exactly, but she added details about the weather and what was happening all around. And things to remember.

"For instance, I wrote something down the other day," she said. "Something that Lois said. Lois and Sylvie came in when Mrs. Green was here and Mrs. Green was mentioning how the berry bushes were growing along the lane and stretching across the road, and Lois said, 'It's like in

"Sleeping Beauty."' Because I'd read them the story. I made a note of that."

Rupert said, "I'll have to get after those berry canes and cut them back."

Enid got the impression that he was pleased by what Lois had said and by the fact that she had written it down, but it wasn't possible for him to say so.

One night he told her that he would be away for a couple of days, at a stock auction. He had asked the doctor if it was all right, and the doctor had said to go ahead.

That night he had come before the last pills were given, and Enid supposed that he was making a point of seeing his wife awake before that little time away. She told him to go right in to Mrs. Quinn's room, and he did, and shut the door after him. Enid picked up the paper and thought of going upstairs to read it, but the children probably weren't asleep yet; they would find excuses for calling her in. She could go out on the porch, but there were mosquitoes at this time of day, especially after a rain like the afternoon's.

She was afraid of overhearing some intimacy or perhaps the suggestion of a fight, then having to face him when he came out. Mrs. Quinn was building up to a display, of that Enid felt sure. And before she made up her mind where to go she did overhear something. Not the recriminations or (if it was possible) the endearments, or perhaps even weeping, that she had been half expecting, but a laugh. She heard Mrs. Quinn weakly laughing, and the laughter had the mockery and satisfaction in it that Enid had heard before but also something she hadn't heard before, not in her life—something deliberately vile. She didn't move, though she should have, and she was at the table still, she was still there staring at the door of the room, when he came out a moment later. He didn't avoid her eyes—or she his. She couldn't. Yet she couldn't have said for sure that he saw her. He just looked at her and went on outside. He looked as if he had caught hold of an electric wire and begged pardon—who of?—that his body was given over to this stupid catastrophe.

The next day Mrs. Quinn's strength came flooding back,

169

in that unnatural and deceptive way that Enid had seen once or twice in others. Mrs. Quinn wanted to sit up against the pillows. She wanted the fan turned on.

Enid said, "What a good idea."

"I could tell you something you wouldn't believe," Mrs. Quinn said.

"People tell me lots of things," said Enid.

"Sure. Lies," Mrs. Quinn said. "I bet it's all lies. You know Mr. Willens was right here in this room?"

III. MISTAKE

Mrs. Quinn had been sitting in the rocker getting her eyes examined and Mr. Willens had been close up in front of her with the thing up to her eyes, and neither one of them heard Rupert come in, because he was supposed to be cutting wood down by the river. But he had sneaked back. He sneaked back through the kitchen not making any noise—he must have seen Mr. Willens' car outside before he did that—then he opened the door to this room just easy, till he saw Mr. Willens there on his knees holding the thing up to her eye and he had the other hand on her leg to keep his balance. He had grabbed her leg to keep his balance and her skirt got scrunched up and her leg showed bare, but that was all there was to it and she couldn't do a thing about it, she had to concentrate on keeping still.

So Rupert got in the room without either of them hearing him come in and then he just gave one jump and landed on Mr. Willens like a bolt of lightning and Mr. Willens couldn't get up or turn around, he was down before he knew it. Rupert banged his head up and down on the floor, Rupert banged the life out of him, and she jumped up so fast the chair went over and Mr. Willens' box where he kept his eye things got knocked over and all the things flew out of it. Rupert just walloped him, and maybe he hit the leg of the stove, she didn't know what. She thought, It's me next. But she couldn't get round them to run out of the room. And then she saw Rupert wasn't going to go for her after all. He was out of wind and he just set the chair right side up and sat down in it. She went to Mr. Willens then and hauled him around, as heavy as he was, to get him right side up. His eyes were not quite open, not shut either, and there was dribble coming out of his mouth. But no skin broke on his face or bruise you could see—maybe it wouldn't have come up yet. The stuff coming out of his mouth didn't even look like blood. It was pink stuff, and if you wanted to know what it looked like it looked exactly like when the froth comes up when you were boiling the strawberries to make jam. Bright pink. It was smeared over his face from when Rupert had him face down. He made a sound, too, when she was turning him over. *Glug-glug.* That was all there was to it. *Glug-glug* and he was laid out like a stone.

Rupert jumped out of the chair so it was still rocking, and he started picking up all the things and putting each one back where it went in Mr. Willens' box. Getting everything fitted in the way it should go. Wasting the time that way. It was a special box lined with red plush and a place in it for each one of his things that he used and you had to get everything in right or the top wouldn't go down. Rupert got it so the top went on and then he just sat down in the chair again and started pounding on his knees.

On the table there was one of those good-for-nothing cloths, it was a souvenir of when Rupert's mother and father went up north to see the Dionne Quintuplets. She took it off the table and wrapped it around Mr. Willens' head to soak up the pink stuff and so they wouldn't have to keep on looking at him.

Rupert kept banging his big flat hands. She said, Rupert, we got to bury him somewhere.

Rupert just looked at her, like to say, Why?

She said they could bury him down in the cellar, which had a dirt floor.

"That's right," said Rupert. "Where are we going to bury his car?"

She said they could put it in the barn and cover it up with hay.

He said too many people came poking around the barn.

Then she thought, Put him in the river. She thought of him sitting in his car right under the water. It came to her like a picture. Rupert didn't say anything at first, so she went into the kitchen and got some water and cleaned Mr. Willens up so he wouldn't dribble on anything. The goo was not coming up in his mouth anymore. She got his keys, which were in his pocket. She could feel, through the cloth of his pants, the fat of his leg still warm.

She said to Rupert, Get moving.

He took the keys.

They hoisted Mr. Willens up, she by the feet and Rupert by the head, and he weighed a ton. He was like lead. But as she carried him one of his shoes kind of kicked her between the legs, and she thought, There you are, you're still at it, you horny old devil. Even his dead old foot giving her the nudge. Not that she ever let him do anything, but he was always ready to get a grab if he could. Like grabbing her leg up under her skirt when he had the thing to her eye and she couldn't stop him and Rupert had to come sneaking in and get the wrong idea.

Over the doorsill and through the kitchen and across the porch and down the porch steps. All clear. But it was a windy day, and, first thing, the wind blew away the cloth she had wrapped over Mr. Willens' face.

Their yard couldn't be seen from the road, that was lucky. Just the peak of the roof and the upstairs window. Mr. Willens' car couldn't be seen.

Rupert had thought up the rest of what to do. Take him to Jutland, where it was deep water and the track going all the way back and it could look like he just drove in from the road and mistook his way. Like he turned off on the Jutland road, maybe it was dark and he just drove into the water before he knew where he was at. Like he just made a mistake.

He did. Mr. Willens certainly did make a mistake.

The trouble was, it meant driving out their lane and along the road to the Jutland turn. But nobody lived down there and it was a dead end after the Jutland turn, so just the half-mile or so to pray you never met anybody. Then Rupert would get Mr. Willens over in the driver's seat and push the car right off down the bank into the water. Push the whole works down into the pond. It was going to be a job to do that, but Rupert at least was a strong bugger. If he hadn't been so strong they wouldn't have been in this mess in the first place.

Rupert had a little trouble getting the car started because he had never driven one like that, but he did, and got turned around and drove off down the lane with Mr. Willens kind of bumping over against him. He had put Mr. Willens' hat on his head—the hat that had been sitting on the seat of the car.

Why take his hat off before he came into the house? Not just to be polite but so he could easier get a clutch on her and kiss her. If you could call that kissing, all that pushing up against her with the box still in one hand and the other grabbing on, and sucking away at her with his dribbly old mouth. Sucking and chewing away at her lips and her tongue and pushing himself up at her and the corner of the box sticking into her and digging her behind. She was so surprised and he got such a hold she didn't know how to get out of it. Pushing and sucking and dribbling and digging into her and hurting her all at the same time. He was a dirty old brute.

She went and got the Quintuplets cloth where it had blown on to the fence. She looked hard for blood on the steps or any mess on the porch or through the kitchen, but all she found was in the front room, also some on her shoes. She scrubbed up what was on the floor and scrubbed her shoes, which she took off, and not till she had all that done did she see a smear right down her front. How did she come by that? And the same time she saw it she heard a noise that turned her to stone. She heard a car and it was a car she didn't know and it was coming down the lane.

She looked through the net curtain and sure enough. A new-looking car and dark green. Her smeared-down front and shoes off and the floor wet. She moved back where she couldn't be seen, but she couldn't think of where to hide.

The car stopped and a car door opened, but the engine didn't cut off. She heard the door shut and then the car turned around and she heard the sound of it driving back up the lane. And she heard Lois and Sylvie on the porch.

It was the teacher's boyfriend's car. He picked up the teacher every Friday afternoon, and this was a Friday. So the teacher said to him, Why don't we give these ones a lift home, they're the littlest and they got the farthest to go and it looks like it's going to rain.

It did rain, too. It had started by the time Rupert got back, walking home along the riverbank. She said, A good thing, it'll muddy up your tracks where you went to push it over. He said he'd took his shoes off and worked in his sock feet. So you must have got your brains going again, she said.

Instead of trying to soak the stuff out of that souvenir cloth or the blouse she had on, she decided to burn the both of them in the stove. They made a horrible smell and the smell made her sick. That was the whole beginning of her being sick. That and the paint. After she cleaned up the floor, she could still see where she thought there was a stain, so she got the brown paint left over from when Rupert painted the steps and she painted over the whole floor. That started her throwing up, leaning over and breathing in that paint. And the pains in her back—that was the start of them, too.

After she got the floor painted she just about quit going into the front room. But one day she thought she had better put some other cloth on that table. It would make things look more normal. If she didn't, then her sister-in-law was sure to come nosing around and say, Where's that cloth Mom and Dad brought back the time they went to see the Quints? If she had a different cloth on she could say, Oh, I just felt like a change. But no cloth would look funny.

So she got a cloth Rupert's mother had embroidered with flower baskets and took it in there and she could still smell the smell. And there on the table was sitting the dark-red box with Mr. Willens' things in it and his name on it and it had been sitting there all the time. She didn't even remember putting it there or seeing Rupert put it there. She had forgot all about it.

She took that box and hid it in one place and then she hid it in another. She never told where she hid it and she wasn't going to. She would have smashed it up, but how do you smash all those things in it? Examining things. Oh, Missus, would you like me to examine your eyes for you, just sit down here and just you relax and you just shut the one eye and keep the other one wide open. Wide open, now. It was like the same game every time, and she wasn't supposed to suspect what was going on, and when he had the thing out looking in her eye he wanted her to keep her panties on, him the dirty old cuss puffing away getting his fingers slicked in and puffing away. Her not supposed to say anything till he stops and gets the looker thing packed up in his box and all and then she's supposed to say, "Oh, Mr. Willens, now, how much do I owe you for today?"

And that was the signal for him to get her down and thump her like an old billy goat. Right on the bare floor to knock her up and down and try to bash her into pieces. Dingey on him like a blowtorch.

How'd you've liked that?

Then it was in the papers. Mr. Willens found drowned.

They said his head got bunged up knocking against the steering-wheel. They said he was alive when he went in the water. What a laugh.

IV. LIES

Enid stayed awake all night—she didn't even try to sleep. She could not lie down in Mrs. Quinn's room. She sat in the kitchen for hours. It was an effort for her to move, even to make a cup of tea or go to the bathroom. Moving her body shook up the information that she was trying to arrange in her head and get used to. She had not undressed, or unrolled her hair, and when she brushed her teeth she seemed to be doing something laborious and unfamiliar. The moonlight came through the kitchen window—she was sitting in the dark—and she watched a patch of light shift through the night, on the linoleum, and disappear. She was surprised by its disappearance and then by the birds waking up, the new day starting. The night had seemed so long and then too short, because nothing had been decided.

She got up stiffly and unlocked the door and sat on the porch in the beginning light. Even that move jammed her thoughts together. She had to sort through them again and set them on two sides. What had happened—or what she had been told had happened—on one side. What to do about it on the other. What to do about it—that was what would not come clear to her.

The cows had been moved out of the little meadow between the house and the riverbank. She could open the gate if she wanted to and go in that direction. She knew that she should go back, instead, and check on Mrs. Quinn. But she found herself pulling open the gate bolt.

The cows hadn't cropped all the weeds. Sopping wet, they brushed against her stockings. The path was clear, though, under the riverbank trees, those big willows with the wild grape hanging on to them like monkeys' shaggy arms. Mist was rising so that you could hardly see the river. You had to fix your eyes, concentrate, and then a spot of water would show through, quiet as water in a pot. There must be a moving current, but she could not find it.

Then she saw a movement, and it wasn't in the water. There was a boat moving. Tied to a branch, a plain old rowboat was being lifted very slightly, lifted and let fall. Now that she had found it, she kept watching it, as if it could say something to her. And it did. It said something gentle and final.

You know. You know.

When the children woke up they found her in bountiful good spirits, freshly washed and dressed and with her hair loose. She had already made the jello crammed with fruit that would be ready for them to eat at noon. And she was mixing batter for cookies that could be baked before it got too hot to use the oven.

"Is that your father's boat?" she said. "Down on the river?"

Lois said yes. "But we're not supposed to play in it." Then she said, "If you went down with us we could." They had caught on at once to the day's air of privilege, its holiday possibilities, Enid's unusual mix of languor and excitement.

"We'll see," said Enid. She wanted to make the day a special one for them, special aside from the fact—which she was already almost certain of—that it would be the day of their mother's death. She wanted them to hold something in their minds that could throw a redeeming light on whatever came later. On herself, that is, and whatever way she would affect their lives later.

That morning Mrs. Quinn's pulse had been hard to find and she had not been able, apparently, to raise her head or open her eyes. A great change from yesterday, but Enid was not surprised. She had thought that great spurt of energy, that wicked outpouring talk, would be the last. She held a spoon with water in it to Mrs. Quinn's lips, and Mrs. Quinn drew a little of the water in. She made a mewing sound— the last trace, surely, of all her complaints. Enid did not call the doctor, because he was due to visit anyway later that day, probably early in the afternoon.

She shook up soapsuds in a jar and bent a piece of wire, and then another piece, to make bubble wands. She showed the children how to make bubbles, blowing steadily and carefully until as large a shining bladder as possible trembled on the wire, then shaking it delicately free. They chased the bubbles around the yard and kept them afloat till breezes caught them and hung them in the trees or on the eaves of the porch. What kept them alive then seemed to be the cries of admiration, screams of joy, rising up from below. Enid put no restriction on the noise they could make, and when the soapsud mixture was all used up she made more.

The doctor called when she was giving the children their lunch—jello and a plate of cookies sprinkled with coloured sugar and glasses of milk into which she had stirred chocolate syrup. He said he had been held up by a child's falling out of a tree and he would probably not be out before suppertime. Enid said softly, "I think she may be going."

"Well, keep her comfortable if you can," the doctor said. "You know how as well as I do."

Enid didn't phone Mrs. Green. She knew that Rupert would not be back yet from the auction and she didn't think that Mrs. Quinn, if she ever had another moment of consciousness, would want to see or hear her sister-in-law in the room. Nor did it seem likely that she would want to see her children. And there would be nothing good about seeing her for them to remember.

She didn't bother trying to take Mrs. Quinn's blood pressure anymore, or her temperature—just sponged off her face and arms and offered the water, which was no longer noticed. She turned on the fan, whose noise Mrs. Quinn had so often objected to. The smell rising from the body seemed to be changing, losing its ammoniac sharpness. Changing into the common odour of death.

She went out and sat on the steps. She took off her shoes and stockings and stretched out her legs in the sun. The children began cautiously to pester her, asking if she would take them down to the river, if they could sit in the boat, or if they found the oars could she take them rowing. She knew enough not to go that far in the way of desertion, but she asked them, Would they like to have a swimming-pool? Two swimming-pools? And she brought out the two laundry tubs, set them on the grass, and filled them with water from the cistern pump. They stripped to their underpants and lolled in the water, becoming Princess Elizabeth and Princess Margaret Rose.

"What do you think," said Enid, sitting on the grass with her head back and her eyes shut—"what do you think, if a person does something very bad, do they have to be punished?"

"Yes," said Lois immediately. "They have to get a licking."

"Who did it?" said Sylvie.

"Just thinking of anybody," said Enid. "Now, what if it was a very bad thing but nobody knew they did it? Should they tell that they did and be punished?"

Sylvie said, "I would know they did it."

"You would not," said Lois. "How would you know?"

"I would've seed them."

"You would not."

"You know the reason I think they should be punished?" Enid said. "It's because of how bad they are going to feel, in themselves. Even if nobody did see them and nobody ever knew. If you do something very bad and you are not punished you feel worse, you feel far worse, than if you are."

"Lois stold a green comb," Sylvie said.

"I did not," said Lois.

"I want you to remember that," Enid said.

Lois said, "It was just laying the side the road."

Enid went into the sickroom every half-hour or so to wipe Mrs. Quinn's face and hands with a damp cloth. She never spoke to her and never touched her hand, except with the cloth. She had never absented herself like this before with anybody who was dying. When she opened the door at around half past five she knew there was nobody alive in the room. The sheet was pulled out and Mrs. Quinn's head was hanging over the side of the bed, a fact that Enid did not record or mention to anybody. She had the body straightened out and cleaned and the bed put to rights before the doctor came. The children were still playing in the yard.

"July 5. Rain early A.M. L. and S. playing under porch. Fan off and on, complains noise. Half cup eggnog spoon at a time. B.P. up, pulse rapid, no complaints pain. Rain didn't cool off much. R.Q. in evening. Hay finished.

"July 6. Hot day, vy. close. Try fan but no. Sponge often. R.Q. in evening. Start to cut wheat tomorrow. Everything 1 or 2 wks ahead due to heat, rain.

"July 7. Cont'd heat. Won't take eggnog. Ginger ale from spoon. Vy. weak. Heavy rain last night, wind. R.Q. not able to cut, grain lodged some places.

"July 8. No eggnog. Ginger ale. Vomiting A.M. More alert. R.Q. to go to calf auction, gone 2 days. Dr. says go ahead.

"July 9. Vy. agitated. Terrible talk.

"July 10. Patient Mrs. Rupert (Jeanette) Quinn died today approx. 5 P.M. Heart failure due to uremia. (Glomerulonephritis.)"

Enid never made a practice of waiting around for the funerals of people she had nursed. It seemed to her a good idea to get out of the house as soon as she decently could. Her presence could not help being a reminder of the time just before the death, which might have been dreary and full of physical disaster, and was now going to be glossed over with ceremony and hospitality and flowers and cakes.

Also, there was usually some female relative who would be in place to take over the household completely, putting Enid suddenly in the position of unwanted guest.

Mrs. Green, in fact, arrived at the Quinns' house before the undertaker did. Rupert was not back yet. The doctor was in the kitchen drinking a cup of tea and talking to Enid about another case that she could take up now that this was finished. Enid was hedging, saying that she had thought of taking some time off. The children were upstairs. They had been told that their mother had gone to Heaven, which for them had put the cap on this rare and eventful day.

Mrs. Green was shy until the doctor left. She stood at the window to see him turn his car around and drive away. Then she said, "Maybe I shouldn't say it right now, but I will. I'm glad it happened now and not later when the summer was over and they were started back to school. Now I'll have time to get them used to living at our place and used to the idea of the new school they'll be going to. Rupert, he'll have to get used to it, too."

This was the first time that Enid had realized that Mrs. Green meant to take the children to live with her, not just to stay for a while. Mrs. Green was eager to manage the move, had been looking forward to it, probably, for some time. Very likely she had the children's rooms ready and material bought to make them new clothes. She had a large house and no children of her own.

"You must be wanting to get off home yourself," she said

to Enid. As long as there was another woman in the house it might look like a rival home, and it might be harder for her brother to see the necessity of moving the children out for good. "Rupert can run you in when he gets here."

Enid said that it was all right, her mother was coming out to pick her up.

"Oh, I forgot your mother," said Mrs. Green. "I forgot about that snappy little car."

She brightened up and began to open the cupboard doors, checking on the glasses and the teacups—were they clean for the funeral?

"Somebody's been busy," she said, quite relieved about Enid now and ready to be complimentary.

Mr. Green was waiting outside, in the truck, with the Greens' dog, General. Mrs. Green called upstairs for Lois and Sylvie, and they came running down with some clothes in brown paper bags. They ran through the kitchen and slammed the door, without taking any notice of Enid.

"That's something that's going to have to change," said Mrs. Green, meaning the door-slamming. Enid could hear the children shouting their greetings to General and General barking excitedly in return.

Two days later Enid was back, driving her mother's car herself. She came late in the afternoon, when the funeral would have been well over. There were no extra cars parked outside, which meant that the women who had helped in the kitchen had all gone home, taking with them the extra chairs and teacups and the large coffeepot that belonged to their church. The grass was marked with car tracks and some dropped crushed flowers.

She had to knock on the door now. She had to wait to be asked in.

She heard Rupert's heavy, steady footsteps. She spoke some greeting to him when he stood in front of her on the other side of the screendoor, but she didn't look into his face. He was in his shirtsleeves, but was wearing his suit trousers. He undid the hook of the door.

"I wasn't sure anybody would be here," Enid said. "I

thought you might still be at the barn."

Rupert said, "They all pitched in with the chores."

She could smell whisky when he spoke, but he didn't sound drunk.

"I thought you were one of the women come back to collect something you forgot," he said.

Enid said, "I didn't forget anything. I was just wondering, how are the children?"

"They're fine. They're at Olive's."

It seemed uncertain whether he was going to ask her in. It was bewilderment that stopped him, not hostility. She had not prepared herself for this first awkward part of the conversation. So that she wouldn't have to look at him, she looked around at the sky.

"You can feel the evenings getting shorter," she said. "Even if it isn't a month since the longest day."

"That's true," said Rupert. Now he opened the door and stood aside and she went in. On the table was a cup without a saucer. She sat down at the opposite side of the table from where he had been sitting. She was wearing a dark-green silk-crêpe dress and suède shoes to match. When she put these things on she had thought how this might be the last time that she would dress herself and the last clothes she would ever wear. She had done her hair up in a French braid and powdered her face. Her care, her vanity, seemed foolish but were necessary to her. She had been awake now three nights in a row, awake every minute, and she had not been able to eat, even to fool her mother.

"Was it specially difficult this time?" her mother had said. She hated discussion of illness or deathbeds, and the fact that she had brought herself to ask this meant that Enid's upset was obvious.

"Was it the children you'd got fond of?" her mother said. "The poor little monkeys."

Enid said it was just the problem of settling down after a long case, and a hopeless case of course had its own strain. She did not go out of her mother's house in the daytime, but she did go for walks at night, when she could be sure of not meeting anybody and having to talk. She had found herself walking past the walls of the county jail. She knew there was a prison yard behind those walls where hangings had once taken place. But not for years and years. They must do it in some large central prison now, when they had to do it. And it was a long time since anybody from this community had committed a sufficiently serious crime.

Sitting across the table from Rupert, facing the door of Mrs. Quinn's room, she had almost forgotten her excuse, lost track of the way things were to go. She felt her purse in her lap, the weight of her camera in it—that reminded her.

"There is one thing I'd like to ask you," she said. "I thought I might as well now, because I wouldn't get another chance."

Rupert said, "What's that?"

"I know you've got a rowboat. So I wanted to ask you to row me out to the middle of the river. And I could get a picture. I'd like to get a picture of the riverbank. It's beautiful there, the willow trees along the bank."

"All right," said Rupert, with the careful lack of surprise that country people will show, regarding the frivolity—the rudeness, even—of visitors.

That was what she was now—a visitor.

Her plan was to wait until they got out to the middle of the river, then to tell him that she could not swim. First ask him how deep he thought the water would be there—and he would surely say, after all the rain they had been having, that it might be seven or eight, or even ten, feet. Then tell him that she could not swim. And that would not be a lie. She had grown up in Walley, on the lake, she had played on the beach every summer of her childhood, she was a strong girl and good at games, but she was frightened of the water, and no coaxing or demonstrating or shaming had ever worked with her—she had not learned to swim.

He would only have to give her a shove with one of the oars and topple her into the water and let her sink. Then leave the boat out on the water and swim to shore, change his clothes, and say that he had come in from the barn or from a walk and found the car there, and where was she?

Even the camera if found would make it more plausible. She had taken the boat out to get a picture, then somehow fallen into the river.

Once he understood his advantage, she would tell him. She would ask, Is it true?

If it was not true, he would hate her for asking. If it was true—and didn't she believe all the time that it was true? —he would hate her in another, more dangerous way. Even if she said at once—and meant it, she would mean it—that she was never going to tell.

She would speak very quietly all the time, remembering how voices carry out on the water on a summer evening.

"I am not going to tell, but you are. You can't live on with that kind of secret."

You cannot live in the world with such a burden. You will not be able to stand your life.

If she had got so far, and he had neither denied what she said nor pushed her into the river, Enid would know that she had won the gamble. It would take some more talking, more absolutely firm but quiet persuasion to bring him to the point where he would start to row back to shore.

Or, lost, he would say "What will I do?" and she would take him one step at a time, saying first, "Row back."

The first step in a long, dreadful journey. She would tell him every step and she would stay with him for as many of them as she could. Tie up the boat now. Walk up the bank. Walk through the meadow. Open the gate. She would walk behind him or in front, whichever seemed better to him. Across the yard and up the porch and into the kitchen.

They will say goodbye and get into their separate cars and then it will be his business where he goes. And she will not phone the Police Office the next day. She will wait and they will phone her and she will go to see him in jail. Every day, or as often as they will let her, she will sit and talk to him in jail, and she will write him letters as well. If they take him to another jail she will go there; even if she is allowed to see him only once a month she will be close by. And in court—yes, every day in court, she will be sitting where he can see her.

She does not think anyone would get a death sentence for this sort of murder, which was in a way accidental, and was surely a crime of passion, but the shadow is there, to sober her when she feels that these pictures of devotion, of a bond that is like love but beyond love, are becoming indecent.

Now it has started. With her asking to be taken on the river, her excuse of the picture. Both she and Rupert are standing up, and she is facing the door of the sickroom—now again the front room—which is shut.

She says a foolish thing.

"Are the quilts taken down off the windows?"

He doesn't seem to know for a minute what she is talking about. Then he says, "The quilts. Yes. I think it was Olive took them down. In there was where we had the funeral."

"I was only thinking. The sun would fade them."

He opens the door and she comes around the table and they stand looking into the room. He says, "You can go in if you like. It's all right. Come in."

The bed is gone, of course. The furniture is pushed back against the walls. The middle of the room, where they would have set up the chairs for the funeral, is bare. So is the space in between the north windows—that must have been where they put the coffin. The table where Enid was used to setting the basin, and laying out cloths, cotton wool, spoons, medicine, is jammed into a corner and has a bouquet of delphiniums sitting on it. The tall windows still hold plenty of daylight.

"Lies" is the word that Enid can hear now, out of all the words that Mrs. Quinn said in that room. *Lies. I bet it's all lies.*

Could a person make up something so detailed and diabolical? The answer is yes. A sick person's mind, a dying person's mind, could fill up with all kinds of trash and organize that trash in a most convincing way. Enid's own mind, when she was asleep in this room, had filled up with the most disgusting inventions, with filth. Lies of that nature could be waiting around in the corners of a person's mind, hanging like bats in the corners, waiting to take advantage of any kind of darkness. You can never say, Nobody could make that up. Look how elaborate dreams are, layer over layer in them, so that the part you can remember and put into words is just the bit you can scratch off the top.

When Enid was four or five years old she had told her mother that she had gone into her father's office and that she had seen him sitting behind his desk with a woman on his knee. All she could remember about this woman, then and now, was that she wore a hat with a great many flowers on it and a veil (a hat quite out of fashion even at that time), and that her blouse or dress was unbuttoned and there was one bare breast sticking out, the tip of it disappearing into Enid's father's mouth. She had told her mother about this in perfect certainty that she had seen it. She said, "One of her fronts was stuck in Daddy's mouth." She did not know the word for breasts, though she did know they came in pairs.

Her mother said, "Now, Enid. What are you talking about? What on earth is a front?"

"Like an ice-cream cone," Enid said.

And she saw it that way, exactly. She could see it that way still. The biscuit-coloured cone with its mound of vanilla ice cream squashed against the woman's chest and the wrong end sticking into her father's mouth.

Her mother then did a very unexpected thing. She undid her own dress and took out a dull-skinned object that flopped over her hand. "Like this?" she said.

Enid said no. "An ice-cream cone," she said.

"Then that was a dream," her mother said. "Dreams are sometimes downright silly. Don't tell Daddy about it. It's too silly."

Enid did not believe her mother right away, but in a year or so she saw that such an explanation had to be right, because ice-cream cones did not ever arrange themselves in that way on ladies' chests and they were never so big. When she was older still she realized that the hat must have come from some picture.

Lies.

She hadn't asked him yet, she hadn't spoken. Nothing yet committed her to asking. It was still *before*. Mr. Willens had still driven himself into Jutland Pond, on purpose or by accident. Everybody still believed that, and as far as Rupert was concerned Enid believed it, too. And as long as that was so, this room and this house and her life held a different possibility, an entirely different possibility from the one she had been living with (or glorying in—however you wanted to put it) for the last few days. The different possibility was coming closer to her, and all she needed to do was to keep quiet and let it come. Through her silence, her collaboration in a silence, what benefits could bloom. For others, and for herself.

This was what most people knew. A simple thing that it had taken her so long to understand. This was how to keep the world habitable.

She had started to weep. Not with grief but with an onslaught of relief that she had not known she was looking for. Now she looked into Rupert's face and saw that his eyes were bloodshot and the skin around them puckered and dried out, as if he had been weeping, too.

He said, "She wasn't lucky in her life."

Enid excused herself and went to get her handkerchief, which was in her purse on the table. She was embarrassed now that she had dressed herself up in readiness for such a melodramatic fate.

"I don't know what I was thinking of," she said. "I can't walk down to the river in these shoes."

Rupert shut the door of the front room.

"If you want to go we can still go," he said. "There ought to be a pair of rubber boots would fit you somewhere."

Not hers, Enid hoped. No. Hers would be too small.

Rupert opened a bin in the woodshed, just outside the kitchen door. Enid had never looked into that bin. She had thought it contained firewood, which she had certainly had no need of that summer. Rupert lifted out several single rubber boots and even snow boots, trying to find a pair.

"These look like they might do," he said. "They maybe were Mother's. Or even mine before my feet got full size."

He pulled out something that looked like a piece of a tent, then, by a broken strap, an old school satchel.

"Forgot all the stuff that was in here," he said, letting these things fall back and throwing the unusable boots on top of them. He dropped the lid and gave a private, grieved, and formal-sounding sigh.

A house like this, lived in by one family for so long a time, and neglected for the past several years, would have plenty of bins, drawers, shelves, suitcases, trunks, crawl spaces full of things that it would be up to Enid to sort out, saving and labelling some, restoring some to use, sending others by the boxload to the dump. When she got that chance she wouldn't balk at it. She would make this house into a place that had no secrets from her and where all order was as she had decreed.

He set the boots down in front of her while she was bent over unbuckling her shoes. She smelled under the whisky the bitter breath that came after a sleepless night and a long harsh day; she smelled the deeply sweat-soaked skin of a hard-worked man that no washing—at least the washing he did—could get quite fresh. No bodily smell—even the smell of semen—was unfamiliar to her, but there was something new and invasive about the smell of a body so distinctly not in her power or under her care.

That was welcome.

"See can you walk," he said.

She could walk. She walked in front of him to the gate. He bent over her shoulder to swing it open for her. She waited while he bolted it, then stood aside to let him walk ahead, because he had brought a little hatchet from the woodshed, to clear their path.

"The cows were supposed to keep the growth down," he said. "But there's things cows won't eat."

She said, "I was only down here once. Early in the morning."

The desperation of her frame of mind then had to seem childish to her now.

Rupert went along chopping at the big fleshy thistles. The sun cast a level, dusty light on the bulk of the trees ahead. The air was clear in some places, then suddenly you would enter a cloud of tiny bugs. Bugs no bigger than specks of dust that were constantly in motion yet kept themselves together in the shape of a pillar or a cloud. How did they manage to do that? And how did they choose one spot over another to do it in? It must have something to do with feeding. But they never seemed to be still enough to feed.

When she and Rupert went underneath the roof of summer leaves it was dusk, it was almost night. You had to watch that you didn't trip over roots that swelled up out of the path, or hit your head on the dangling, surprisingly tough-stemmed vines. Then a flash of water came through the black branches. The lit-up water near the opposite bank of the river, the trees over there still decked out in light. On this side—they were going down the bank now, through the willows—the water was tea-coloured but clear.

And the boat waiting, riding in the shadows, just the same.

"The oars are hid," said Rupert. He went into the willows to locate them. In a moment she lost sight of him. She went closer to the water's edge, where her boots sank into the mud a little and held her. If she tried to, she could still hear Rupert's movements in the bushes. But if she concentrated on the motion of the boat, a slight and secretive motion, she could feel as if everything for a long way around had gone quiet.

JOHN METCALF is a writer, editor and critic who lives in Ottawa. "Forde Abroad" is one of a sequence of stories that will be published under the title *Travelling Northward*. It won the gold award for fiction at the Twentieth Annual National Magazine Awards.

MARK ANTHONY JARMAN was born in Edmonton and is a graduate of the Iowa Writers' Workshop. He has been published in *Queen's Quarterly*, *Hawaii Review* and *Passages North* and his first novel, *Salvage King Ya!* appeared in 1997. He now teaches English at the University of Victoria.

RAMONA DEARING has contributed poetry to *Fiddlehead* and is currently working on a collection of stories. She is a CBC reporter in St. John's, Newfoundland.

CYNTHIA FLOOD is the author of two collections of stories, *The Animals in Their Elements* and *My Father Took a Cake to France*, and was awarded the Journey Prize in 1990. She is now at work on a novel and a third group of stories.

DAVID HENDERSON has lived in Vancouver, Boston and San Francisco, and currently makes his home in Ottawa. "Remembering Manuel" won the silver award for fiction at the Twentieth Annual National Magazine Awards.

CHRISTIAN PETERSEN lives in Williams Lake, BC. He has been published widely in literary journals and magazines and recently completed a collection of stories set in the Cariboo/Chilcotin region. "Horse from Persia" is based on a true event.

ALICE MUNRO is one of Canada's best-known writers and has won the Governor General's Award three times. Her most recent collection of stories is *Open Secrets*, and her novel, *Lives of Girls and Women*, was recently made into a movie by the CBC. She lives with her husband in a small town in Ontario.

DOUGLAS GLOVER is the author of three story collections and three novels, including the critically acclaimed *The Life and Times of Captain N*. His stories have appeared in *Best American Short Stories*, *Best Canadian Stories* and *The New Oxford Book of Canadian Stories*, and criticism has appeared in the *Globe and Mail*, *Montreal Gazette*, *New York Times Book Review*, *Washington Post Book World* and *Los Angeles Times*. He teaches creative writing at Vermont College.